June 2007

All the Best!
Enjoy!

Anna Bell Blake

Only the Heart Know's...

~

by
Annabell Blake

AuthorHouse™
1663 Liberty Drive, Suite 200
Bloomington, IN 47403
www.authorhouse.com
Phone: 1-800-839-8640

© 2007 Annabell Blake. All rights reserved.

No part of this book may be reproduced, stored in a retrieval system, or transmitted by any means without the written permission of the author.

First published by AuthorHouse 5/31/2007

ISBN: 978-1-4343-1494-9 (sc)

Printed in the United States of America
Bloomington, Indiana

This book is printed on acid-free paper.

To all women who have ever been in love...

"Whatever our souls are made of, his and mine are the same..."
Emily Bronte

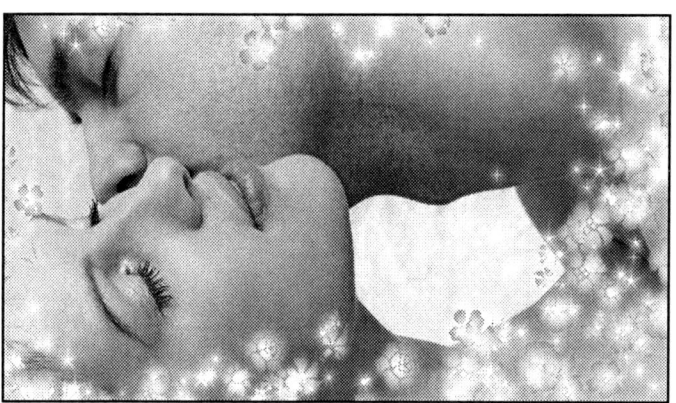

Chapter 1
I Think I'm Falling in Love With You

"I think I'm falling in love with you." That's all Larry said while the children ran playing and swinging, laughing and giggling around us. I looked at him, and those blue eyes lit up like a Christmas tree. He seemed so proud to have said those words out loud. He smiled as if he had been keeping a secret for a very long time. It felt as if he wanted me to understand how wonderful this feeling was for him. The warmth of the summer breeze and the words he'd said seemed to linger in the air. It was one of the sweetest and most unexpected moments of my life.

Had I really heard what Larry just said to me, or was I daydreaming? I sat down, my head spinning and my heart pounding, and all I could do was get up and walk over to watch my child play with the other kids. I excused myself by saying, "It's time to go in and get ready for bed."

As I was walking away, I thought, *How could this man be in love with me? We're both married and have families. Hell, I'm even friends with his obsessive wife!* Life had just thrown me a curveball. It had been ten years since anyone besides my husband had shown any interest in my forty-something butt. I went home and got my little boy ready for bed. While getting Levi's bath, I just could not stop thinking about Larry. My intuition told me to be careful, but my soul told me to enjoy the moment. I decided to go to bed and sleep on it. Everything would look different in the morning light. My life had changed; everything and everyone in my life would be forever different.

Chapter 2
The Chase Begins

It was 8:25 a.m. Monday morning.

Ring! Ring!

"Levi, help me find my cell phone!" I yelled as I was driving entirely too fast to get him to school on time.

"Here Mama, I found it!"

"Hello?"

"Well, good morning!"

"Who is this?"

"It's me, Larry. I just wanted to call you and tell you to have a wonderful day and let you know I'll be thinking about you!"

I grinned. "I can't really talk right now. I'll talk to you later."

"Okay. I'll call you back in a little while. Have a great day! Goodbye!"

Oh my God! Did he just call me and say what I think he said?

"Who was that, Mama?" asked Levi.

"Oh … nobody. Give me a kiss and have a good day at school." I drove away confused and feeling somewhat guilty. *What's happening here? What did I do to make Larry feel this way about me?* I had a lot of questions and very few answers.

As I was driving to my workout, I thought, *What am I doing? What are Larry's intentions? Is this a game for him? Could it be a midlife crisis?* Again, I had unanswered questions. I decided to forget about Larry for now and go in for my morning workout. *A good hard sweat always helps clear the mind.* I hit the floor hard. My girlfriends were already breaking a sweat. The music was playing and I was getting my heart rate up. Suddenly all I could think about was that silly phone call. Every song that played made me think of him, and those thoughts drove me to work even harder as they ran rampant through my mind. *I can't even consider this guy. It isn't right; he isn't right. He isn't even my type. I'll be able to blow him off. Hell, I've blown off bigger fish before. I don't really even like him. He's a car salesman, for God's sake! And his wife's just dirty and greedy. Hell's bells! I'm married to a handsome lawyer who gives me everything. So what's the problem? There is no problem. The next time I talk to Larry, I'll tell him to back off, that's all. No way I'll ever fall in love with him. Okay. That's it. Next time he calls, I'm setting him straight.*

Ring! Ring! I stopped my workout and looked to see who was calling. *Larry … Well, I just won't answer it. I'll just let it go to the answering service. He won't leave a message. I have to get out of here. I'll go home and call him and straighten this whole thing out.*

I had to call him. I hadn't been in this sort of dilemma for years! As soon as I got home, I dialed the number.

A sweet, young voice answered. "Maloney's Auto Sales."

"Yes, may I please speak to Mr. Larry Williams?" I said with a trembling, faint voice.

"Just a moment please."

Now I had seconds to hang up, pretend none of this had happened, and just ignore the whole thing.

"This is Mr. Williams. Can I help you?"

That's an interesting question. Yes, you can help me! Stop making me feel like a silly schoolgirl! "Hi, it's Laura."

His voice seemed to brighten. "Hi! How are you? I can't stop thinking about you. Did you hear what I said to you last night?"

"Yes …"

I could almost hear him smiling over the phone. "Listen, I understand you're looking for donations for your PTO. I think I can help. I talked to my boss, and he said I could choose a nonprofit to help out from our department. So I thought since you're the big PTO president I'd make a donation. What do you think?"

"That would be great," I said, "but you don't have to do that. Your children go to another school. Why don't you give a donation to them?"

"Because I want to help you. And besides, I want you to tutor my son. He isn't doing well in school. Reading is his main problem, and you know how my wife is—no patience. You work so well with him, and besides, he likes you. I'll pay you if you help me out."

"I'll think about it," I said.

"Okay." His voice grew quiet. "Do you have any idea how beautiful you are?"

"Well, I have to go now," I said, flustered. "I'll talk to you later. Goodbye."

"Goodbye, beautiful!" he said.

"He thinks I'm beautiful!" I smiled at my dog. "Did you hear that, Moonlight?" I didn't understand why in the world he would want to give my PTO a donation when his children went to another school. Agnes, his wife, would have a mad fit. She was the greediest person I'd ever met. The thoughts began to race again. *I wonder how much money Maloney's will donate? We do need the funding. Our account's getting low. And it'll be kind of fun to see the look in Agnes's eyes when she finds out he's giving money to my son's school! Okay, I'll play along for a while. It just might be fun. Besides, we aren't hurting anyone. Let's see what Mr. Williams does next. I'll bet he doesn't give a penny to my PTO.*

Chapter 3
The Allure

There was magic in the air—and mystery. I think women evolve into a higher self when they feel admired and loved. I'd been enticed into an attraction that was forbidden. I had more confidence and a lighter step in my walk. Just living became more inviting. I was like Sleeping Beauty when she first woke up. Even after marrying and having a child, I was still in the age of innocence.

I had to get back to my normal daily life, whatever normal was. After all, I had many responsibilities. I thought I had a good grip on the world. The only difference was that I was now sharing a small part of myself with Larry. I was willing to speak to him only on the phone (several times a day) and see him in public settings with family and friends. It was as if we were in our own little world. Our time was special. We talked about everything: our dreams, the children, the sun in the sky, our work. The topic didn't matter. We just had a connection. It was as if Patrick and Agnes were not part of the equation. We were happy just to see each other or hear each other's voices. We had so many inside jokes that we could laugh for hours.

And there was something else. He always wanted to get naked. Of course, I'd just say "Yeah, right, in your dreams." I wouldn't cross that line with him. He wanted to, but I just couldn't. I tried to keep our relationship on the up-and-up. Have you ever felt that the chain of events in your life is not accidental? That's how I was beginning to feel about Larry. Everything happens according to an inner need. I wondered whether I was beginning to need Larry.

He finally pulled it off. He came to me one day at home with a thousand-dollar check for the PTO. The way he grinned while walking up the pavement made it seem as though he owned the world.

"I've got something for you," he said, reaching into his pocket. He handed me the check.

"Thank you, Larry. You have no idea what this means to me and the school," I said.

"I'm glad I could help. Are you guys going to John and Kelly's tonight?"

I looked down, feeling foolish. "Yes."

"Well, I'll see you there, sweetie!" And with a wink, he was gone.

Later that evening, all the neighbors got together over at the Millers' for a summer barbeque. We all had young families, and it was easier to get together at each other's homes to relax, visit, and let the kids play than it was to go out. We always had a good time. On that particular evening, I spent more time getting ready than I normally did; after all, I had to look as good as I could for Larry. I also spent more time on the dishes I brought. They just had to be good; with hope they would be the best. I baked a couple apple pies and made a fresh green salad. I had a couple bottles of wine as well. I thought I might need a glass or two. On the way over, Patrick said, "You look very nice tonight, Laura."

Good, I thought. *Maybe Larry will think so as well.*

Annabell Blake

These get-togethers with friends and neighbors were getting trickier. The ladies always formed one group and the men another. I was beginning to feel awkward around Agnes. Besides, she was so wrapped up in buying and spending that she probably would never in a million years notice what was going on before her very eyes. I had always thought of her as dirty and hard. You know—the type that you just want to put in the bathtub and give a good scrubbing though you know it won't do any good. You just end up with dirty water and a big lump of mud, so what's the use? The way she talked drove me crazy! She had a way of breaking everything down to how many "bucks" she had spent on this and that, most of which she and her family didn't need. Poor Larry; she was going to put him in the poor house. But you know what? That wasn't any of my business; that was Larry's problem. I just wanted to enjoy his sweet talk and attention. I liked it—maybe too much.

Later that evening I heard Larry talking to Patrick. "So how's it going, old man?" he asked Patrick. I thought, *I don't like that. No, I don't like that at all. Who's he to call my husband an old man?* Patrick was older than the rest of us by almost twenty years, but he was still my husband. *I'm not going to let Larry get away with that,* I thought. I slowly walked over and sat down on Patrick's lap, then gave him a big kiss and a hug.

Patrick grinned broadly. "Wow! Sweetheart, what was that for?"

"Oh I don't know," I said, smiling up at Larry. "I just felt like giving you a kiss." I could tell by the look in Larry's eyes that he was not pleased.

I'll bet he wishes I was kissing him instead.

Larry got up and went to get a drink. I needed one too. He and I were the only ones who really knew what had just taken place, and I felt the need to get away. I picked up my wine glass and went searching for some new company. I found another group of ladies around the front of the house. Thank goodness Agnes wasn't there. I found comfort and solace in chatting about the mundane. Everything was okay, and I stayed away from Larry the rest of the night. I noticed that he was getting drunker and that his attitude was getting worse. I figured I'd have gotten drunk too if I'd had to go home with Agnes at the end of the evening.

Later that evening I found myself swinging on a porch swing with my "old-man" husband. He wasn't showing love to me with kind words or gazing into my eyes, but it was okay. I was safe, and I admired him. I don't think he would ever tell another's man wife he was in love with her. I knew he didn't think about love or romance. Sometimes … well, sometimes I wished he would just notice me a little bit more. I guess after ten years of marriage there wasn't much mystery left. We were comfortable, like an old pair of jeans. Together, we had a handsome little boy, a nice home, a beach house, a generous retirement, and a college fund for Levi. You could say we were safe and comfortable. But where did all the magic go? Maybe it was all in our little boy. Or maybe there just wouldn't be any unless we made it ourselves.

The next morning I received a phone call from Larry. "Hello?" I said.

"Well, hello beautiful! How are you this morning?"

"I'm fine, and you?"

"I saw you two sitting on the porch swing last night. I watched you talking, all comfortable and cozy and sweet.

Only the Heart Know's...

What do you guys talk about? I guess you know it drove me crazy; I wanted to grab you and take you away!"

It burst out of me. "Larry, this is ridiculous! I'm married, you're married, and I'm not in love with you!"

"Laura, you know you love me! We're soul mates! You're all I think about! I can't sleep. I wouldn't even go home if it weren't for the kids and the chance of seeing you. What am I going to do? I'm crazy in love with you."

Sadly, I could hear the pain and fear in his voice. I really wanted to help him, but how could I? "Well, I guess you should think about making some changes; maybe a divorce would be a start."

"Do you think you could meet me for lunch? I … I just need someone to talk to."

"Okay, but just to talk," I said.

"That's fine. Meet me at the Cowboy's Steakhouse. It's quiet there at lunch, and no one will know us," he said.

"What time?"

"Eleven," he said.

"I'll be there," I said softly. "Goodbye."

"Goodbye sweetie, and thank you."

Chapter 4
Getting To Know You, Getting To Know All About You

Well, here I go, I thought. Talking on the phone or seeing each other in public with family and friends was one thing, but now I was heading into a whole new dimension. The truth is I was hooked; I did kind of like him. I didn't know how or why. Maybe it was the light in his eyes, the secrets of his heart, or his longing to live a full life. I needed someone to shake me and wake me up! Larry was a middle-aged man with a nothing to offer. *He isn't special. Hell, if I were buying a horse, I'd look at his teeth and say 'no way!'* He was short and had a wide, flat butt, and I won't even mention his belly. He was as pale as ivory on the piano. But here I was, going to meet the most average man alive. Need I say I was excited?

When I pulled up to the restaurant, there he was, waiting for me. I smiled at him and saw many possibilities. Sometimes life can be a daring adventure or nothing at all. Today—well, today I was going for the adventure! I was going to listen to Larry—*really* listen. I wanted to get answers to all my questions. Maybe I could help him and he could help me. He opened my car door, and he reached out to squeeze my hand while bending to kiss me on the cheek. "I'm so glad you decided to come. I've waited a long time to talk to you seriously."

We went into Cowboy's and were seated in a booth next to a big picture window. I was extremely glad. I looked away. Outside I saw the sun shining, and I watched the cars go by. We both ordered coffee and ice water.

Then we began to talk.

It started with his first bad marriage. He married under the gun and entirely too young. His first wife had trapped him, he said. She'd told him she was pregnant and that they had to get married. He had always dreamed of having a large family, so he'd married her. It turned out she had never been with child and had just told him that to get him to marry her. After he found out the truth, he lost all interest in her and they divorced. A few years later he fell head over heels in love with a well-educated debutante. They were passionately in love. They married in style and moved to the city. Because she had the better-paying job, they decided he would be the stay-at-home father when their babies were born. She would continue in the business world. Eventually they thought they would be blessed with children, but that day never came. A few years passed, and still there were no children, so Larry decided to find out why.

After just a little searching, he found birth control pills in her purse. To quote him directly, "It got ugly." Of course he confronted her, and once more the truth came out. She didn't want to have children, and she never had. His first wife had trapped him with a make-believe pregnancy, and the second had told him she wanted children, but didn't. Poor Larry! He'd gone from one extreme to another. And if that weren't enough, during marriage counseling he'd found out his wife was gay! She actually had a girl friend and was in love!

I didn't know whether I should laugh or cry. Needless to say, Larry found himself single once again.

The third time's a charm—or is it? He had been working hard at Maloney's Auto Sales and was now making a nice living as the manager. He was slowly getting over wife number two and having sex with everyone he could get his hands on. It was once again time for marriage and children. The problem was that he was dating a wonderful redheaded flight attendant whom he adored and a dental assistant who was—well, let's just say *easy*. He really liked Kathryn, the flight attendant, but she didn't believe in premarital sex. The dental assistant, Agnes, would have sex with him three or four times a day. It wasn't a difficult decision for him.

It seemed to me that Larry was still on the rebound at that time. After all, the love of his life had just left him for another woman. He should've married the nicer girl. If he had, everything probably would've turned out differently. Later in the conversation I found out the flight attendant he had been dating was a very good friend of mine. She was one of the kindest, most intelligent, and most beautiful women I've ever known. I could hardly believe he'd picked Agnes over Kathryn. *How sad,* I thought. *I guess he didn't think he was worthy of a good woman.* It was all starting to add up.

The waitress came over and filled up our cups again with coffee. "Would you like to order lunch now?" she asked.

"Yes," I said while excusing myself. "I'll have whatever he orders." I quickly walked to the ladies room and checked my cell phone. *No messages; good.* I looked in the mirror. *What am I doing here?* I checked my lipstick and hair. *Everything's good.* I had to call Kathryn. I remembered her talking about a Larry a few years ago. *Boy, it's a small world. I wonder what she thinks of him now. Do they still talk?*

Upon returning to the table, I asked, "What did you order for lunch?"

"Well, I know you like to eat healthy food, so I ordered us grilled chicken and a salad. Is that okay?"

"Great! I would've ordered the same. When do you have to get back to work?"

"Oh, I have plenty of time. I can take all afternoon if I want to. I'm the boss," he said while laughing.

Great. No timeline. "Well, I have to get home soon," I said.

The waitress brought our lunch and I was relieved. *We'll eat and I'll go home; no damage done.*

As we ate, Larry continued with his testimony. He was nearing the present date, and I was getting nervous. Sometimes ignorance really is bliss. I used to think there were no mistakes in life; that God put people in our lives for a reason. So here I was, sitting across the table from my neighbor's husband, listening—just listening.

Larry's voice snapped me from my thoughts. "Laura?"

"Yes?"

"Are you happy?"

Happy? "Yes, I guess so … yes, of course I'm happy.

"Well, I'm not. I haven't been for years. I love my children, and work's going well, but things are not working out with Agnes. In fact, I'm miserable. She spends all my money, doesn't take care of the kids, and the house is a wreck. I'm embarrassed when I'm out in public with her. All she does is talk, talk, talk, but guess what? She doesn't have anything to say." He paused and looked at me. His mood changed. "How many times a week do you and Patrick make love?"

"What? That's none of your business, Larry!"

"Okay, you're right, I'm sorry. I was out of line. It's just that Agnes and I don't anymore. I'm not interested in her. She's put on so much weight ... she doesn't take care of herself at all." He looked at the table, shaking his head. "What am I going to do about her?"

"Get a divorce, Larry! Right away if you're that unhappy."

He went on to tell me that he was planning a divorce and was hiding as much money from her as he could. He had a special hiding place in the attic so the lawyers couldn't find it.

Wow! Now that's planning! I guess experience is paying off here. Can't say I blame him. If I were that unhappy, I'm sure I'd get out too.

Then, just when I didn't think he could tell me more, he did.

Only the Heart Know's...

Remember Kathryn, my flight attendant friend? Larry had been talking to her on the phone and they had been seeing each other during his lunch hour. I thought, *He really is going to leave Agnes. But if he's involved with Kathryn, what's he doing calling me and asking me to meet him?* I knew I had to call Kathryn, and soon.

Larry finally got to the present date. "Laura?"

"Yes, Larry," I said, feeling emotionally exhausted.

"The truth is, I really love you. And if you were to tell me there was any chance of us getting together ... well, I—"

"You know, Larry, I'm friends with your wife, not to mention Kathryn. If you had made different choices, well, maybe one of my best friends would be my neighbor, and ... God, I can't *believe* this, Larry! My marriage is hard at times, I confess, but you and I could *never* work."

I stopped. I was feeling sad and angry with this greedy little man. I looked out the window. Everything was still. He reached over and held my hand. I looked down at our hands, then up at him. "I have to go now," I said. "I have to go think." I pulled my hand away as I reached for my purse. He rose and walked me outside. The sun was so bright that I put on my sunglasses before searching for my keys.

"Don't go," he said. "Let's drive to the park and talk. We can just sit together ... *be* together."

"You better get back to work, Larry. Maybe we can talk later." I closed my door and he waved as I drove off.

I drove home as quickly as I could with the radio playing and my mind racing in every direction. I wasn't halfway home when my cell phone rang. "Hello?"

It was Patrick. "Hello sweetheart! What's for dinner tonight?"

"I thought we'd eat out tonight, if that's all right with you," I said.

"Great! I'll be home early! Goodbye!"

"Goodbye." I felt just awful … and guilty. *Thank God he didn't ask where I was.* Now I had to go out to eat again, but this time with my husband and son. I didn't feel so well. *Ring! Ring!* I jumped, startled by the phone. *My God, who's calling now?* "Hello?"

"Hi, sweetie!" *Larry!* "I just wanted you to know that I'm thinking about you and that I love you dearly."

"Okay, Larry. I'm thinking about you too. Can we talk tomorrow?"

"Sure. And thanks for having lunch with me. I really enjoyed it. Goodbye."

"Goodbye." *I just need to get home. I'll take a hot bath and I'll be fine.* Just then a silly tune popped into my head: *I'm gonna wash that man right out of my hair!*

Chapter 5
The Garage Sale

As I waited patiently for my morning coffee to brew, I turned on the television to catch the local news and weather. What I heard on the broadcast was not good. A little three-year-old girl a few minutes up the highway from us in a trailer park had been badly beaten and raped by her thirteen-year-old babysitter and his friend. When the boys finished with her, they'd thrown her through a picture window, leaving her to die. She'd been found by a neighbor and taken to the nearby hospital. She was in critical care and in a coma. The Channel 6 News reporter said that if Lilly recovered and her mother was found to be unable to care for her little girl because of her alleged prostitution and methamphetamine abuse, she'd be placed in a foster home. At this time, her father's identity was unknown.

Patrick and I had wanted to add a little girl to our family, but I'd had a miscarriage last winter. It simply wasn't meant to be. Here was another special little girl, only she has been beaten and left for dead. *Oh my God*, I thought. *I have to do something for her.* After dropping Levi off at school I went shopping and filled a basket with stuffed animals, books, toys, and soft, cuddly clothes for Lilly. When I was finished, I wrapped it all up in cellophane and put a big yellow bow on the basket. I enclosed a card with some money. I hoped she'd live, and I hoped she'd be loved someday soon. Now all I had to do was find a way to get my care basket to her. *Maybe I can even meet her. I'll give her a hug and show her some love and compassion.*

While I was wrapping my basket, Agnes called. She wanted to know whether she and Elizabeth could use the pool that afternoon. "Sure," I said. I didn't care. I loved Elizabeth; I would spoil her. She had her daddy's eyes. Agnes never gave her any attention. Elizabeth and I would do girl things, such as combing our hair and polishing our nails. She loved to play with make up, and what little girl doesn't? Sometimes I would run her a bubble bath—her favorite thing to do. She would giggle and play and ask lots of questions, such as "Why do girls wear lipstick?" Or she'd hold up a bottle of scented lotion and ask, "What's this for?" What a sweetheart.

Agnes came in from the pool to get a drink and cool off from the sun. That's when she saw my basket for Lilly. "Wow! Who's that for?"

I told her what I had heard on the news. "I wanted to do something, so I filled a basket for her. Actually, I need to get it to the hospital."

"You know, I have a good friend who could drop it off for you. Sarah's a critical care nurse there."

"You wouldn't mind asking her?"

"No problem. I'm sure she'd love to give Lilly your gift."

I agreed. Later that afternoon when Agnes left to go home, she took the beautiful basket with her.

A few days later I was driving by Agnes's house. She was out in her garage setting up for her garage sale. I stopped and asked whether Sarah had taken my basket to Lilly.

She smiled. "Yes! Lilly had gotten a lot of gifts and balloons, so Sarah laid it in with all the others. I'm sure she'll get it."

"Okay." I pulled away to drive home, but I had a funny feeling in my stomach as though I had been sucker-punched. *She's lying; I can feel it*, I thought to myself. What Agnes had said wasn't quite right. The way she had said it and the look in her eyes—again, I could just feel it.

I tried to forget about Lilly and the care basket. I had followed the story on the news. She had awakened from her coma and was out of critical care. There was a new, loving family waiting to take Lilly home.

Later that weekend the neighborhood was having its annual fall garage sale. I made my rounds, seeing what everyone was selling and buying. It was lots of fun. I had given Levi ten dollars. He would have a blast buying used toys. I enjoyed watching everybody, drinking coffee, and visiting.

Agnes took the sale very seriously. She was in it to make "that buck," as she said, and I have to hand it to her, she had a lot of stuff. I finally made my way to her house. I started looking around, and that's when she got really nervous. She obviously didn't want me around. But as a rush of people showed up, she got busy and I started looking again. I was looking through her box of stuffed animals when I saw them—the stuffed animals I had bought for Lilly! I was aghast. *How could she steal from a wounded, beaten little girl!?* Then I went on a mission. Sure enough, I found the books and the clothes too. Everything I had bought for Lilly was in her sale. I wondered what she'd done with the money in the card.

I looked over at her as she collected money from the people who had come to her sale. They were lined up five deep. I sat everything down and walked away. I was sad for myself and for Lilly, but mostly for Agnes—and Larry. I never said anything to her—I didn't know what to say—but after that I looked at her through entirely different eyes.

Chapter 6
Losing Control

Life is an illusion, and Larry was beginning to take over my illusion. It happened slowly at first. Then suddenly he was everywhere. He would show up at the gas station when I was filling up. When I was taking my walks, he would drive by and stop. When I drove my son to school, there he was. He would even call me when I was getting my nails and hair done. What's funny about it all is that I enjoyed the attention. He filled a loneliness I didn't even know I had. I wanted him in my life more and more. Patrick was fading into the background, and Larry said it was just a matter of time before he filed for a divorce.

Fall came, and the leaves were more beautiful than they had been in years. We were again invited to a neighborhood party. There would be a big campfire and hot cider for the kids. I dressed in a new pair of hip-hugger jeans and a fall sweater. There was a chill in the air that night, and the moon was full. It was the perfect fall evening. Family after family showed up, and only Larry and Agnes and their children were late.

I made my usual rounds, making small talk and drinking my hot toddy. I walked over to the fire to get warm, and there he was. He took my breath away. I had just had my first celestial moment, and it was divine. He wore a blue jean jacket with a flannel shirt and a pair of Levi's. I have never in my life seen such a handsome man. I will never forget that moment. Larry looked up at me and winked. Later he whispered sweet nothings in my ear. He even wrapped a blanket around me to keep me warm. I was so happy I wanted to cry.

Months passed and Larry and I continued to talk on the phone. We ran into each other here and there. We got together at neighborhood gatherings, and we continued our friendly little flirting sessions. His favorite line to whisper in my ear was, "Want to go somewhere and get naked?" I'd always laugh it off with "In your dreams." Sometimes we caught a minute or two alone, but it was always strangely awkward, probably because we weren't free. We also knew our feelings were strong, and I felt more than guilty enough with just the phone calls and all the flirtation.

The snow fell throughout an entire night in early December, so the schools were closed. I was on the phone with one of my best friends, Jessie. We were chit-chatting about the kids and the weather when all of a sudden I heard a snow blower in my driveway. It was Larry! I said, "Jessie you won't believe who's in my driveway clearing the snow."

"Who?"

"Larry!"

"Why would he be clearing the snow off your driveway? Laura, if his wife finds out, she'll kill you!" Jessie said.

"I know. I'll explain the whole thing to you when we meet to let the kids sled at the park."

"Explain what?" A smile crept into her voice. "You can't do this to me! You have to tell me *now*, Laura!"

"I can't. Levi will hear me, and anyway I don't know if I know myself. Let's talk later, okay?"

"Okay, but I want to know what's going on. First he gives you a thousand dollars for the PTO, and now he's clearing your driveway? Where's Patrick?"

"He's away on business. I'll talk with you later."

I hung up and quickly ran to put on a robe and a pair of boots. Then I opened the door, and there was Larry, clearing my sidewalk. I yelled, "What are you doing?"

He stopped. "What does it look like I'm doing?"

"What about Agnes?"

He grinned. "Don't worry, Sweetie. I cleaned off four other driveways just so I could clear yours."

"But why?"

"You have to ask? I love you; that's why. These little things are the only way I can show you how much I care."

I gave up. "Is there anything I can get you?"

"Sure. Make me some hot coffee and I'll come in to warm up."

"Okay." I went back in. *He's coming in! I have to get dressed and fix my hair! A little lip gloss will help, and I have to make coffee. I wonder how long he'll stay? What will I tell Levi? I'll figure something out.*

I was in the kitchen making coffee when I heard my dogs barking and Larry coming through the front door. He was covered in snow—entirely covered! "Get out of those wet clothes and I'll put them in the dryer while you have your coffee."

He grinned. "Gladly."

I laughed. "You'd do just about anything to strip in front of me, wouldn't you?"

"You're right! Where's that coffee? What are you up to today?"

"Well, I thought I'd meet Jessie and the kids over at the park so the boys could go sledding. I think the dogs would love it too."

"Sounds like fun. I wish I could go with my kids."

I looked at him. "So why didn't you just go on home for coffee and dry clothes?"

"Agnes doesn't make coffee." He smiled. "And besides, I wanted to see you."

We visited for about thirty minutes. He drank three cups of coffee and played with Levi. He told Levi he was the neighborhood snow blower. Levi thought that was cool. It was a fun morning that was full of surprises.

I blushed when I thought of Larry. I thought I was losing control.

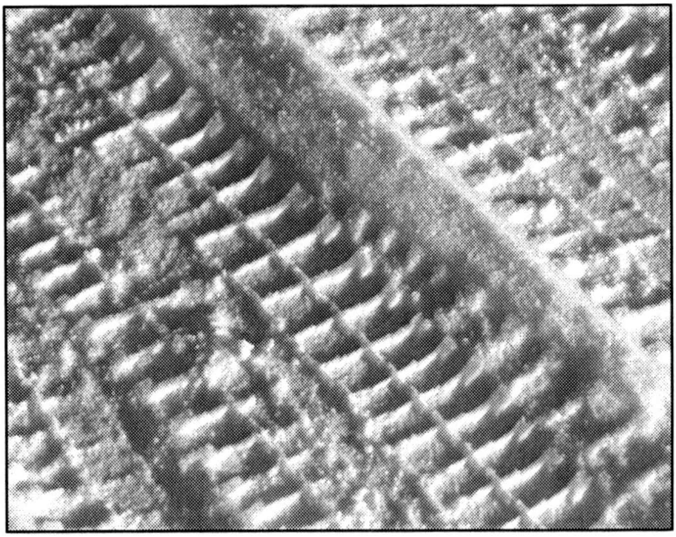

Chapter 7
Sharing My Secret

Levi and I picked up Jessie and the kids and we headed for the park to sled and build snowmen. The snow was soft and fluffy, and the streets were clean and quiet. The only noise was the crunching of the snow under the weight of Patrick's truck. Everything sparkled in the sunlight. "I just love snow days," Levi said. The truth is that I do too. The children get to stay home and play and drink hot chocolate with lots of marshmallows. It's almost like Christmas. The kids were excited; they were all bundled up and ready to play. We arrived at the park safely and the kids all piled out laughing and planning the perfect sleigh ride.

Jessie looked at me. "Okay, what's up?"

"I don't know what you mean," I said.

"Don't give me that. You have to tell me *everything*, sister! Now, what's going on between you and Larry? You know I'm not stupid. I see the way you guys look at each other. So what's going on? Tell me."

"All right, can you keep a secret?"

"Of course I can! Do you have to ask?"

"Well, Larry and I have been talking on the phone every day, several times a day. In fact, I could set my watch by his calls: 8:35, 10:30, 1:15, and 4:45. He pops in on me almost everywhere I go—even in my dreams. He said he was unhappily married and was planning a divorce. I was just trying to be a good friend and—Oh, Jessie! What am I going to do about him? I think I'm falling for him!"

Jessie started laughing. "I *knew* it! I just *knew* something was going on! You'd have to be blind not to see it. First off, Laura, nobody gives money to a school their children don't go to, and secondly, his awful, dirty, butt-headed wife! Nobody can stand her! Everyone just tolerates her for him." She paused. "Oh, but what about Patrick? Well, you guys could always just have an affair.

"Jessie, he says he's in love with me."

"Have you guys ... " She hesitated.

"No! No, we haven't ... I ... I can't go that far. I mean, he would in a heartbeat! He says he dreams about it! But Jessie, we're both married! It would just be too wrong for me. I don't think I could live with myself. You know, I'm not sorry I'm falling for Larry. I'm just really sorry it's happening *now*. The timing is wrong. On the other hand, I've never felt so alive," I said with some shame.

"So what are you going to do? You know we all go through stuff like this at one time or another."

I shook my head. "Well, I guess I'll just ride this out to the end. As long as he knows I won't cross the line, well, I think I can live with myself."

Jessie smiled. "Well, I think it's great, Laura! Enjoy yourself! You only live once. If you ever need to talk, you know where I am."

There's nothing like sharing a secret with a good friend. The kids came back to the truck all snowy and cold. We loaded them up and headed in for dry clothes and hot chocolate. It was funny, but I felt much better since I'd shared my secret.

Chapter 8
My Christmas Eve

Christmas Eve was my night. I love Christmas; it's a special time of year when everyone feels young and excited. I had started the tradition of having an open house every Christmas Eve. All my neighbors and friends would come over. What excitement! We would eat, drink, and exchange gifts. The kids really loved the festivities. When it was time, we would get online to see where Santa was delivering his gifts. If he started getting close, we would hurry the kids off to bed. Of course there was also singing and putting out birdseed for Santa's reindeer. It was the one of the times of the year I could shower my friends with love and attention. Patrick loved it too. He would greet everyone at the door and get kisses from all the pretty ladies as they passed under the mistletoe. It would take me weeks to get everything ready: the tree, the decorations, the food, and of course, the gifts. Christmas was wonderful and a lot of fun. Unfortunately, this Christmas would be a reminder of how fragile life can be.

It all began with a late afternoon phone call. I was dressed and putting the finishing touches on the food and decorations so everything would be perfect for my party. I had Christmas music playing, the fireplace was lit, and the food smelled great. How could anything go wrong? The phone rang. "Can somebody get that?" I yelled, too busy pulling the ham that Larry had given me out of the oven to take the call.

"Laura, it's for you," Patrick said solemnly. "I'm so sorry. So sorry—"

"What?"

"Just answer the phone, Laura."

It was the nursing home. Grandma was failing. They said I needed to get there as quickly as possible and that she could pass at any moment. I dropped everything. "Patrick, you have to stay here and manage the party without me. Grandma needs me. I have to go."

He looked at me. "Let's cancel the party so I can go with you."

But I shook my head. "No, no ... we can't do that ... all this food ... everyone expecting a Christmas Eve party ... all the kids ... our friends, neighbors ... let's not ruin Christmas for them."

"Laura, I can't do this without you," he said.

Only the Heart Know's...

"Yes. You can; and you will. Everything's ready. Just do this for me, okay?"

"Okay. But what am I going to tell everyone?"

"Tell them to have a Merry Christmas. If I'm missed, tell them I got called away on family business." I ran out the door.

It's strange how courage shows up just when you need it most. It was Christmas Eve, and guess what? It was snowing a soft, beautiful snow. The song "White Christmas" filled my mind. Then suddenly I was a little girl watching Grandma pull her Christmas Eve ham out of the oven. I can still smell the ham and see her smiling. God, how I loved to see her beautiful smile! She could light up an entire room with that smile. I began remembering other times we'd spent together as I drove the forty-five minutes to see her.

On one Easter my dog Skipper stole the neighbor's ham. The Millers weren't the sharpest tools in the shed when it came to common sense. That Easter they had laid their frozen ham out on their back porch to thaw. My part-beagle mixed-breed mutt smelled it and searched it out. What a find for her! She was in doggie Easter heaven. She dragged that ham over to Grandma and Grandpa's house and dined on it for days. During this time she began to swell up like a balloon. We couldn't figure out why until one day when the neighbors came knocking. Sure enough, Skipper had the ham in the backyard, and she'd eaten two-thirds of it. That dog was never the same again. She was now a full-figured girl. We laughed and laughed over that disappearing ham.

As I pulled up to the nursing home, I remembered one more thing. Grandma's mother, my great-grandmother, Ma, had passed away on Christmas Eve ten years earlier. I was with Ma along with my grandmother, mother, and aunt when she passed. I guess Christmas Eve was magical. It seemed that all the women in my life whom I loved dearly wanted to go to heaven on Christmas Eve.

Only the Heart Know's...

I walked into her room and she was laboring to breathe. Her once beautiful body lay wasted away to nothing. I reached down to hold her and whispered that I was there. Softly, I told her everything was going to be all right and gently reminded her of how much I loved her. But it was time for her to let go. Everything was finished. Her life was completed. "Go see your mom and dad and grandpa," I said. "It's Christmas! Go be young and alive in heaven! When you turn around, I'll be there too." Tears were steaming down my cheeks. *God this is hard. How can I live without her?*

The matriarch of the family was dying. When she opened her eyes I could see that she was comforted and that she understood. She asked me for a drink and I reached for the plastic cup near her bed, but it had a sponge on a stick in the water. The nurse came in and explained that I should lay the sponge on her tongue. I did so several times. She was very thirsty. As I was helping her, I thought about Jesus hanging from the cross. He'd been thirsty, too. The Roman soldiers had given him a drink from a sponge as well, but it had been soaked in vinegar; the things we think about when we are scared and trying to be strong can be strange. When she was finished drinking, I sat with her and held her hand. It was getting harder and harder for her to breathe, and I now understood the term *death rattle*. The end was near. My tears flowed uncontrollably. Other family members and a priest came to pay their respects. I left the room for a moment.

I stepped into the dining room and asked for a cup of coffee, then sat down alone and stared out the window to watch the falling snow. Just then my cell phone rang. It was Patrick. All my friends were enjoying Christmas Eve at my house. In my grief and sadness I had forgotten. Patrick passed the phone around and I talked to Jessie and a few of my friends. I sent my regrets and wished them all a very merry Christmas. *They'll find out soon enough*, I thought. *Let them have a wonderful Christmas.* I wondered whether Patrick hadn't already told a few of my friends about Grandma.

Then my little Levi got on the phone. "Mama, where are you? Why aren't you here with Daddy and me? You're missing all the fun!"

"I know," I said, just barely holding myself together. "Mommy will be home soon. Grandma needs Mommy right now. You be a good boy. You help Daddy and try to get to bed early. Remember, Santa's coming."

"Okay Mama, but can you hurry home? Did you know it was snowing out, Mama? We're going to have a white Christmas! Goodbye, Mama. I love you!"

"I love you too, sweetheart." I felt terribly sad. As I hung up the phone, I was inconsolable.

Larry and his family arrived at my party, and it didn't take long for Agnes to ferret out the truth of my situation. Of course she shared her information with Larry.

Being Larry, he went and asked Patrick, "So where's Laura tonight?"

"She had to go south to see her grandmother. They don't think she'll make it through the night. Sad, isn't it?"

"Oh, just awful! Is there anything I can do?"

"No, not right now. Laura just wanted everyone to have a nice Christmas. She'll be fine. She's strong. Thanks anyway."

Larry mingled for a while and then announced that he had to go be Santa's helper, meaning he had toys to put together. He said Agnes should stay and enjoy herself and that he'd see her at home.

Hours passed, but it seemed like days. As visitors and relatives came and went, I sat with Grandma. Sometimes I sat in the hallway on the floor just outside her door. When the time came, I wanted to be close. I was exhausted, and my eyes were stinging from all the crying. I just wanted all the pain and grief to go away. When I least expected it, my cell phone rang. "Hello?"

"Laura, it's Larry. Are you all right?"

"No ... no, I'm not." I began to cry. "My grandmother is dying."

"I'm coming down there. You need me."

Still sobbing, I said, "You can't come down here ... the kids ... Agnes ... Christmas. It's impossible, Larry! No! Don't come down! I'll be fine."

He sounded defeated. "Laura, I really hate this. I want to be with you. I love you."

"I know. There will be a time for us Larry—someday. My Grandmother needs me right now. Do you understand?"

"Yes," he said. "Remember, I love you, sweetie, and I'm thinking about you. How am I going to get through Christmas without knowing if you're all right?"

"I'll be fine—really. Enjoy your kids. I have to go now."

A few hours later, Grandma died. *Merry Christmas, Grandma. Tell everyone hello for me and let them know that I'll see them soon. You're young and beautiful again! Smile for me, Grandma! Smile! I love you! What a beautiful smile she had.*

Chapter 9
The Day After

It was Christmas morning! Levi woke up excited and with anticipation. "Santa's been here! Mama! Daddy! Wake up!"

After just a few hours of restless sleep, I realized this was the first morning of my life that I'd awoken without my Grandmother living. *Oh my God, help me have the strength to get through this day.* Patrick got up and quickly brewed coffee. I spent a few minutes in the bathroom, rinsing my face with cool water. My eyes were all puffy and red. *Oh, I have a headache. It's Levi's Christmas, so I need to pull myself together and get in there.*

"Hurry Mama! I can't wait to open my gifts!" Levi shouted.

I tried to sound happy. "I'm coming, sweetheart." I walked into the family room and saw all the gifts. I forced a smile. "Boy, you must've been a very good boy this year! Santa left you so many presents!"

"You too, Mama! Look at all *your* presents!"

Patrick handed me my coffee with a reassuring smile. "Are you going to make it?"

"I'll try," I said. Christmas morning had begun.

After every package was opened and Levi was off playing with his new toys, Patrick and I had time to talk. "We really outdid ourselves this year," he said.

"Yes. We always say we're going to cut back, but we never do."

"Laura, what can I do for you? What would make you feel better?" He could see by looking at me that the death of my grandmother had left me empty and shaken. I must have looked awfully sad sitting there in my pink robe and clutching my coffee mug tightly so I wouldn't shake so much with grief.

"I'd like to get out of here. Let's tear down the Christmas tree, put away all the decorations, load the car, and head to Florida. I think a change of scenery would do us all a world of good."

Patrick smiled. "And when do you want to do this?"

"Now!" I said. "Right now!" I turned to look down the hallway. "Levi, would you like to go to Disney World?"

"Really, Mama?"

"Yes, really. Go pick out your favorite toys and get your suitcase out. We're leaving today, so get ready."

A few hours later, after the tree was down and the suitcases were in the car, we dropped the dogs off at the doggie resort and took off for Florida!

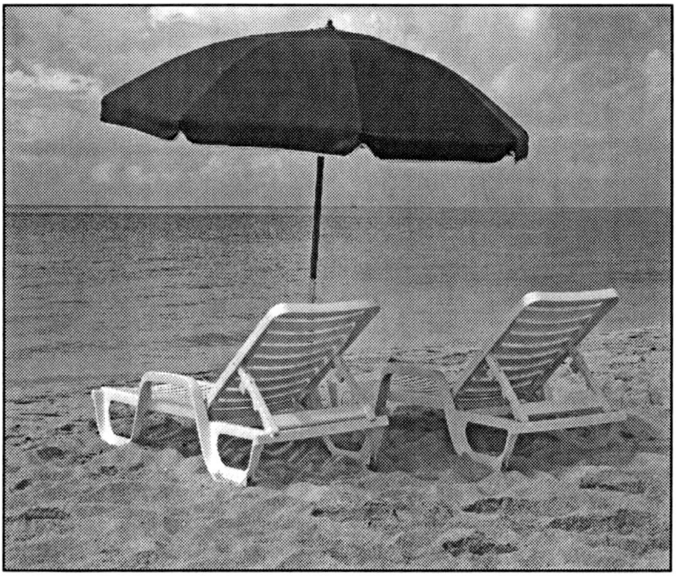

Chapter 10
Reflection and Restoration

After leaving the snow of the Midwest, Florida was refreshing. The sunshine and the salty air alone lift the spirits and feed the soul. Our beach house, which was really just a two-bedroom condo, was beautiful. The colors were so inviting: corals, blues, greens, and yellows. Our other home was decorated with your typical neutrals: browns, creams, sage, soft pink, and gold. Every time I walked into our Florida home, I sighed with relief. I could relax and re-energize. That was what I needed—rest, and lots of it.

We spent days on the beach, and the weather was beautiful and warm. We had a special place with a big umbrella and two big lounge chairs. Levi loved to build sandcastles and ride the waves as the tide came in. Sometimes I'd get up and walk the shore for hours. I made peace with my loss. Looking out at the sea and feeling the warm, salty air on my face was good for reflection and resolution. Levi was a big help too. Some days we would rent kayaks and explore neighboring islands. What fun we had finding shells and discovering new sea animals and birds together! How wonderful it was to see life through a child's eyes!

Patrick—well, he was just Patrick. He didn't understand the feeling of loss I had over losing Grandma. But to me it was much more than that. There had been a lot of loss that year. First both grandpas passed away, then Patrick's mother died, and now I was dealing with Grandma's death. I was down for the count. I had a terrible sense of loss over all of them. Grandma's death just pushed me over the top. Patrick just kept reminding me that he was a Vietnam vet and had seen so much death that it didn't affect him. He was also a recovering alcoholic and had not been making his AA meetings for a few years. When he made his meetings, he was a much better man to live with. When he wasn't making his meetings, he could become very controlling, unbearable, harsh, and at times cold. And if I couldn't share my pain and grief with my husband, then whom could I share it with? *My God!* I thought. *How could he live and not feel pain and loss!* He just didn't get it, and he never would. I was very grateful for Levi. He helped me through the hardest time of my

Only the Heart Know's...

life, and God bless him, he didn't even know it. Levi was a gift—a true, heaven-sent gift.

We made our trip to Disney World and Levi had a terrific time. I'm glad we decided to go. Getting away for a few weeks was a good idea for everyone. As we headed back home, I wondered how everyday life would be without the queen bee of the family with us. I missed her; I really missed her. But life does go on ... .

Hmm ... I thought. *I wonder what Larry's been up to ... No good I'm sure. Oh, that dirty little boy! What am I going to do with him? Hmm ... I wonder.*

Chapter 11
Everyday Life

My pet dogs, Moonlight and Polly, were sure glad to see the family when we picked them up from the doggie resort. I felt good about leaving them there; they always seemed well cared for and relaxed when we arrived to get them. Home just wouldn't be complete without our dogs. Levi started back to school and Patrick gladly returned to work. I was involved in the domestic bliss of cleaning house and being the best mother and wife I could be. I was also tutoring Mark, Larry's little boy, who was having trouble with reading and spelling. His progress was slow but steady, and I enjoyed working with him. I was also working hard in the elementary school. I was asked to help out with fifty-eight kindergartners.

The principal, Mr. Woods, asked me to come in and help some of the needy kids. As life would have it, they ended up helping me. Even with Levi and Patrick, I was still feeling lonely and sad from the recent losses. The kids filled me with love and laughter. I can't thank God enough for the opportunity to spend time at the school with the kids.

I used to go down to the nursing home several times a week and spend a great deal of time taking care of Grandma and Grandpa. I enjoyed being there for them, but of course all that changed with Grandma's death. After that I was spending time with about sixty kids. Oh, the energy of youth! What a contrast from the nursing home! The beginning of life and the end of life are both special. It's all the living in between that's challenging.

Months passed, and I was working and taking care of my family. Life was good. Larry was still relentless with his phone calls and popping in when I least expected him, but it was getting harder for him to talk to me because I was so busy. He finally started calling me at work, which wasn't good because I was working with the students. He also showed up at a few of my PTO meetings and functions. That worried me. *What if someone noticed?* I thought. Larry said I had given him no choice, and I knew he was a determined guy. He kind of reminded me of Napoleon Bonaparte, whose actions came from forces deep within his will. Like Napoleon, Larry was a person who would fight for what he wanted without regret. *Oh my God! Larry has turned into my little Bonaparte!*

I was beginning to feel the toll on my body from all the work and added stress. Along with working, I was also the president of the PTO and was on the library committee. West Side Elementary needed a new library with books, shelves, lighting, tables, and chairs, not to mention new computers, technology, and a completely redecorated and updated library. All of that would take money, so I was asked by the library board to help by writing grants and running a few fundraisers. God was calling and knocking and asking me to contribute. All I could do was say yes. Although the stress and work was mounting, I was feeling more and more run down.

I was so fatigued that even Larry noticed. It might have been simply because I didn't have as much time for our friendly little phone calls. I could still set my watch by those calls. The first call of the day was always at 8:35 a.m. It was the same conversation every morning: *Good morning, beautiful! I'm thinking about you, and I hope you have a great day! Any chance we can meet for lunch?* Blah! Blah! Blah! I wasn't up for all his foolishness. I was either really tired or in the depths of depression. All I knew was that I wanted to sleep.

Chapter 12
Something Is Wrong

A few months passed and the workload remained the same. My fatigue level was at an all-time high. I was exhausted! The only difference was that now, for the first time in my life when I wasn't pregnant, I had a hard, round stomach. Something was wrong.

I finally made an appointment with Dr. White, and it didn't take him long to send me to a specialist. Dr. Von was the bomb! He was wonderful and kind, and he explained everything to me completely. It's kind of funny, because as nice as he was, he reminded me of Frankenstein. I think this was because of the way he walked due to his big, flat feet. He had very broad shoulders and a very dry, dark sense of humor. He was not the kind on man you would expect to be a gynecologist. He told me that I had grown a couple of tumors in my uterus and that they were probably benign because they had grown so fast. But we had to get them out as soon as possible just to make sure. He also thought that these tumors were the reason I had miscarried my little girl. "So how soon could you have surgery? Possibly in the next few days?" asked Dr. Von.

No, that isn't going to work, I thought. "Patrick is out of town on a business trip. I'll have to call your office and let you know," I said.

"Laura, we can't wait too long. It would be in your best interest if we got these out as soon as possible. Do not delay. I'll be waiting for your call," said Dr. Von.

As he turned to walk out the door, I giggled. Dr. Frankenstein is going to operate on me, I thought to myself while smiling. I think his bedside manner, along with the way he looked, kept me from thinking about the seriousness of the surgery.

A few weeks after seeing Dr. Von, I was in the hospital, having surgery. He removed an eight-pound tumor and a couple of three-pound tumors from my body. After the operation, Dr. Von recommended a complete hysterectomy just to be safe. Patrick gave the okay, and the next day I woke up very sore but very relieved. All the tumors were benign. What a relief! It was time to go home and spend a few weeks in bed. Then I would go into physical therapy to regain my strength. The tumors had drained me of all my energy. Now that they were gone, I would soon get back to normal, living pain free again.

Only the Heart Know's...

During all the time I was sick, Larry wanted to be with me. He explained to me that on the morning of my operation he'd parked outside the hospital. He sat in his truck, smoked, drank coffee, and said a few prayers. He thought that if he couldn't be with me, he would at the very least be near me. He also told me he thought about going into the hospital and taking Patrick and my Dad out for lunch in the cafeteria, but he was afraid he wouldn't be able to hold himself together. He also admitted that the day of my operation was the longest day of his life.

At one point he looked up and saw Patrick and my Dad getting in their car to leave, so he took the opportunity to go inside the hospital and ask how I was doing. The nurse asked whether he was family. He thought for a moment, wishing that he could say he was my husband. Shaking his head, he said, "I'm Laura's brother, John."

The nurse smiled. "Well, you just missed your Dad and Patrick. Laura's doing fine. The tumors were all removed and the doctor is performing her hysterectomy. She'll be under for a couple more hours. You can wait in the waiting room if you'd like. Your dad and brother-in-law should be right back."

"Okay, thank you," Larry said. While walking back out to the truck, he thought of all the time we had missed together and about how we could have had beautiful children. He silently prayed: *Please God, just let her be all right. I love her, and I need her. Please take care of my Laura.*

After I came home, Patrick hired a nurse for a while to help me recover. Just taking my daily bath and changing my nightgowns were hard enough. Sometimes I would sit up and eat my meals and drink hot tea from a tray. On pretty spring days I would sit outside under an apple tree for an hour or two and read. It was good to be alive. My spirits were getting better, and I was feeling like my old self again.

It was during this time that Larry would stop by and bring me flowers, books, and sweets. On some days we would lie in bed together for hours and watch old movies. He loved to brush my hair and rub my neck and hands with lotion. I enjoyed watching him; he was very caring and thoughtful. He made me smile. As he would say, "It's my job to make you happy."

He told me about all the anguish he went through during my operation. He cried when he spoke of it. Of course I had no idea, but I wasn't surprised. The very depth of his love showed in his eyes and in his soft, loving voice. This was truly the turning point of our relationship. I believed we were meant to be together. Larry had finally shown me the way. With Larry's visits, my recovery went quickly. That's what being in love does for you.

Chapter 13
Summer Loving

Soon, spring turned to summer, and my pool was open once again. The neighborhood kids were all back, swimming and splashing. It was wonderful to see everyone! I was back, too—still swollen, but basically back to normal. It didn't take long for Agnes and the kids to come over. She carried a huge beach bag and one of those super-size soft drinks from a convenience store. She had a stack of gossip magazines, too. I wouldn't spend money on trash magazines, but if someone else has them and is willing to share them, well, I'll read them for fun.

There we all were, the mommies and our kids, enjoying the summer. Of course we all talked about the kids, school grades, and our husbands. But Agnes was the worst. She was hateful toward her kids, and the things she would say about Larry were just shameful. I cringe just thinking about it. She kept telling us over and over how much she hated Larry and how he spoiled the kids, played too much golf, and worked all the time. The only reason she stayed with "that S.O.B." was for the money. Not to mention she didn't want to go back out in the world and get a new man because of "All those blowjobs and sex and everything!"

I'd never heard a woman talk like that before—so hard and coarse. *God, if Larry only knew*, I thought. *Then again, maybe he does. Maybe that's why he's leaving her.* She'd lie there by my pool for hours telling us how she didn't have to cook or clean or do anything. *Maybe*, I thought, *but an occasional bath and pedicure would be nice. You might even run a brush through that stringy hair.* I know she had no idea how awful she sounded or looked. The other ladies and I just rolled our eyes at each other as she spoke. Larry was right. She talked and talked and talked and had nothing to say!

I asked her once if she ever felt guilty about being so lazy and letting her house go. Being Agnes and having no scruples, she said, "Well, you know I simply have to lie out in the sun every day, weather permitting." She then hastily added, "And of course, Larry knew that when he married me. Besides, he would do anything to keep me happy." She sounded like a barking bitch. *Hmm. Could it be love? Yet she hates him, so what do I care?* Larry had said he hated her too. He would be leaving her soon, and that would be the end of that.

At the end of the day, Patrick phoned to tell me he was working late and wouldn't be home for dinner. *Great! I don't have to cook!* I looked at my son. "Levi, would you like to go to a drive-through tonight? Your daddy won't be home for dinner."

Only the Heart Know's...

"Sure Mama, whatever you want to do," Levi said happily.

Just then, Agnes, who was still lying around my pool seven hours later, invited Levi and me over for a cookout. "Larry's grilling out tonight. Would you guys like to come over and eat with us?"

I hesitated. "Okay, Agnes. Are you sure it will be all right with Larry?"

"Sure, come on over anytime," she said, finally getting up to go home. "I'll see you in a few. Thanks for the beautiful day."

I followed her to the door. "Is there anything I can bring?"

She shook her head. "No. See you later."

An hour later and all cleaned up, Levi and I walked over to Agnes and Larry's for dinner. As we reached the backyard, I saw Larry out on the back porch grilling hamburgers and hotdogs. "Hi, sweetie!" he yelled.

I smiled up at him. "Hello, Larry."

Levi ran off to join the kids on the swing set. "I heard you were coming over for dinner," Larry said, "so I ran to the store and got you some veggie burgers. I know how much you like them." He grinned, pleased with himself. "Help yourself to a glass of wine." It was sitting on the table.

"Oh, I'd love some," I said.

All of a sudden, Agnes came barreling through the screen door, yelling at her son. "Mark! Damn it! You left the upstairs in a mess! You get your little ass in here and clean it up! *Right now!*" she screeched.

My God! The rage in her voice!

"Now Agnes, calm down," Larry said. "What's wrong?"

She wheeled on him, her finger extended. "You wouldn't understand! You *never* understand! He made a huge mess with his toys!" she shouted frantically. "It will take me *hours* to get everything back in place!"

Larry quickly reached his boiling point. "Well, if you wouldn't buy so many goddamn toys, we wouldn't have that problem! One or two cars would be enough, but no! You have to buy several hundred of the damn things! And if you buy Mark and Elizabeth toys, why *can't* they play with them? What are you saving them for?" He sighed, as if resigned. "Agnes, they're just toys. Just calm down. I'll clean everything up later." He reached for the wine bottle. "Here, have a glass of wine and sit down and visit with Laura." He looked disgusted.

Of course, the last thing I wanted to do was sit there with Agnes and listen to her nonsense about Mark's toys. *Life's too short to be involved in this conversation.* She had just a few too many obsessive problems to deal with. Spending time with her was a waste of time and energy.

Still, I didn't leave, and it wasn't long before Larry served dinner. The children were up on the porch eating and laughing, and Larry and I were watching each other closely. Agnes had finished the bottle of wine and moved

Only the Heart Know's...

on to the next bottle. After dinner I helped Larry clean up.

Just then the neighbor lady from across the street came around the corner, announcing that the new ice cream parlor had opened. "Would anyone like to go and then maybe go to the park?"

Well, of course all the kids wanted ice cream, and Agnes—well, she would never, *ever*, pass up a chance to spend money and indulge in a few extra calories. Larry passed, saying he had to clean up after dinner and then head upstairs to clean up Mark's mess. I said I had overeaten and would have to pass as well. So Agnes loaded up the kids, and off they went to get ice cream and then visit the park.

Suddenly, Larry and I were alone. We were standing in the kitchen just looking at each other. I don't remember who moved first, but there we were, in each other's arms, kissing fervently and making passionate love to one another. Larry made love to me time after time after time. It was unbelievable! Neither of us gave a thought to getting caught, nor did we care. I'm not sure where we started or where we finished. It seemed to last an eternity. We really *were* meant to be. Larry kept saying over and over how much he loved me. It was pure bliss—pure heaven on earth, just like I had been dreaming. I *like* dreaming.

Early the next morning, I awoke feeling happy, fresh, and young. I giggled at the thought of what had happened last night. I'd never experienced anybody quite like Larry. I could still feel his hands on my body, and I could still taste his kisses. I walked around in a daze. Patrick left for work and Levi was on his way to school.

I'd just sat down to drink a hot cup of coffee and daydream about Larry when he phoned. "Laura, we belong together. Let's do something about it. Leave Patrick. I'm leaving Agnes right away. I have to be with you, Laura. I have to be with you for the rest of my life." He paused, and then his emotions got the best of him. "My God, Laura, I had no idea two people could be like we were last night! We're more than soul mates; we're *life* mates."

"I know," I said. "I know. Do you have any guilt?"

He responded quickly. "No. Laura, I could never feel guilty for loving you." Hesitancy crept into his voice. "Can you meet me later?"

I smiled. "Yes. Yes, Larry, I would *love* to see you."

We made plans to meet, and I went to shower and get ready.

Later that morning we met and discussed our plans for the future. He looked extremely handsome. I just gazed at him. *Those blue eyes, that's what it is. And his scent! My God, why didn't I notice it before?* Maybe I had noticed it subconsciously. He smelled clean and woodsy all at the same time. My life had completely changed. Larry had been making plans a lot longer than I. He had already found us an apartment to use as our little love nest until we were free.

I listened to him talk, but it was as if it wasn't me. I seemed to be looking down on these two people. Yes, they were in love, and yes, they belonged together, but they both had spouses. We had done a terrible thing by making love to each other when neither of us was free. I had turned down a road that I was not familiar with, and it was a very dumpy road. Plainly and simply, I was having an affair with my neighbor. Never in my wildest dreams did I think this could happen to me.

That summer was the best I had ever had. Larry would tell work and his wife he was playing golf, but we were always together. We spent time looking for a house. We also furniture shopped, and sometimes we headed to the apartment for an afternoon delight. This is when I started calling Larry my dirty little white boy. He was very pale and had blue eyes and blonde hair. I have olive skin, dark brown hair, and green eyes. He called me his Indian squaw, and I called him my dirty little white boy! On some days, we would lie in bed for hours. "A perfect fit," Larry would say. "Like a hand and a glove." We both wondered why it had taken us so long to meet. He would often ask, "Do you believe in miracles, Laura?" Before I could answer, he'd say, "Well I do. We're a miracle, and I love you, Laura."

Several times that summer, he sent Agnes and the kids out of town to visit her sister for long weekends. We would go to artsy little folk towns and walk around holding hands. We were the all-American couple. We would shop, drink margaritas, and even look for wedding rings! Afterwards, Larry would want to go home and lock down his house. He'd run around putting all of Agnes's pictures face down so we didn't have to look at her. Then we would make love in the bed he shared with Agnes! I thought it was a little strange, but he enjoyed it.

Only the Heart Know's...

Once, we saw Agnes's awful, tropical-flower-print full-figured bathing suit lying on the floor. Just for laughs, I got in one leg and he got in the other! We fell onto the bed and laughed and giggled until tears were streaming down our cheeks. Nothing in that house was sacred to Larry. He wanted to make love in every room, including the showers, the bathrooms, and the steps leading upstairs. At times when we were in the kitchen making ourselves something to eat, he would occasionally grab me and put me on the countertop or the dinner table and make wild, passionate love to me. We were extraordinarily happy! He said he wanted to remember me everywhere in his house. Oh, the memories.

Evening at my house took on a whole new light. When Patrick was out of town, which was often, I would put Levi to bed early. Later I would slip outside to the pool, drop my robe, and enjoy a skinny-dip. I would play my stereo on low, listening to soft rock and swimming while looking up at the sparkling clusters of stars in the sky. I could see the steam rising from the pool and causing a majestic, beautiful splendor. The water droplets looked like little glistening diamonds as they fell back into the water. As I swam, I wondered whether Larry would see me. I sure wanted him to.

As I swam and enjoyed the music, I heard a familiar whistle. It was Larry. "Laura, did know your breasts stand up perfectly when you swim?" he whispered.

I laughed. "I guess I've never given it any thought."

"You know, that's one of the things I love about you!"

"What, my breasts?"

"Yes!" His tone turned angry. "Agnes's are so big and hang so low that they don't respond to anything."

"Well, you don't have to worry about that anymore, do you?"

His mood lightened and he laughed. "No. Can I join you?"

"Sure! But what about Agnes?"

"Oh, I gave her a couple sleeping pills. She's out for the night," He said. Then he slipped out of his clothes and joined me in the pool. We had an evening of pure ecstasy under the starry night.

Chapter 14
The Dog Days of Summer

After spending a wonderful afternoon with Larry at our apartment, I headed off to pick up Levi from a friend's house. It was a beautiful day, and I was singing and smiling all the way home. When I got home, Agnes called and asked if Levi could come over and play with Mark. She also wanted to know if I knew anything about a pugapoo—a mixed-breed dog that is a mix between a pug and a poodle. She had seen a pugapoo puppy at the pet store while she was out shopping that day. She really wanted the dog, so I told her I'd be over in a few minutes to talk to her about it. In the meantime, I phoned Larry and told him what his wife was up to.

"No way is she going to get that dog!" he said.

"But Larry, think about it; you're leaving her anyway, and now she'll have a new puppy to distract her."

"You're right. When she calls me and asks about the puppy, I'll hesitate; then I'll say yes. Okay, sweetie. Oh, by the way, you were terrific today! I can still smell your perfume all over me. I just love it, sweetie." His voice softened. "I love you, Laura. I'll be expecting her call."

A few minutes later, I was over at Agnes's house. Levi ran into Mark's room and began playing with his many toys. Agnes was on the computer, shopping again after an entire day of shopping. She had shopping bags everywhere. I said, "My God, Agnes, what are you going to do with all this stuff?"

"Whatever my kids don't use, I'll sell on eBay. Then she got up and showed me a stack of clothes with tags still attached that she had hidden from Larry. Then she laughed. "You know, Mark has over a hundred and forty shirts, not including his T-shirts."

Who in God's name needs that many shirts? I thought. *He's only six years old!* I laughed. "Well, on the upside, I guess he'll outgrow them before he can wear them, and just think—you won't have to do laundry for over a hundred days!"

She didn't think my comment was funny. She sat down on the couch with a big soft drink. "So what do you think about a pugapoo?"

"Hmm, I don't really know anything about them, but if you want one, what's stopping you?"

"Well, it's Larry. We haven't been getting along very well lately, and he says I don't take very good care of the house or the kids. If I add a puppy, it just might push him over the top."

"Well, why don't you call and ask him?" I said reassuringly.

She brightened. "You know, he *is* at work, and it's hard for him to say no to me when he's working, I could always say it's for the kids. You're right. I'll call him right now." She rose to use the phone in the kitchen, smiling like the cat that had just eaten the canary.

After her call she came running into the living room, laughing. "He said yes, Laura! I wonder who the fuck he's sleeping with?" She kept saying, "That was too easy! He must be doing someone! He just has to!"

I thought, *If you only knew ...*

Then she yelled for the kids and loaded them back up in the red minivan for another shopping trip, this time to get a new puppy and all the supplies to go with it.

Agnes came home later with her new pugapoo. It was cute, but it would not be my choice of a new pet. To top it off. Larry hated the dog; it wasn't too bright, and of course,

Agnes didn't train him. I heard he was having accidents all over the house, sometimes in their bed. That gave Larry the excuse to sleep on the couch or with the kids. The new dog, Stanley, caused more problems and more drama for the Williams family. Larry wanted out even more.

Chapter 15
Larry's Sister, Joanne

A few weeks later, Joanne, Larry's sister, came for a visit. She was fair and blonde and had blues eyes, just like Larry. I loved her instantly. She was kind and nice, and she loved Larry's children. She was also noticeably angry and disappointed with Agnes. She asked if I'd ever seen Agnes brush Elizabeth's hair or fix anything for the kids to eat. She said she'd never known such a lazy, despicable woman. "Have you seen their house? It's such a mess! How do they live like that? And why does Larry put up with her? I know, I know—it's the quick blowjobs. At least that's what Larry said. She's a blow*h*ard all right."

What? I'll have to ask him about that.

Joanne also told me Agnes was causing great conflict between Larry and her parents.

"There's a surprise," I responded. Agnes was only out for herself. Her focus was all about her and how much she could buy or eat and drink. Words like *overindulgent* and *sloth* came to mind when I thought about her. I tried to comfort Joanne, and I explained to her that I was sure there would be some changes in the near future.

One Saturday afternoon while everyone was swimming and hanging out at my pool, Joanne came down for a while. It was nice to share my day with her and Larry and all the neighbors. We all ignored Agnes and just went about our day. Larry grilled out for all of us. Everyone pitched in a few dishes. We all enjoyed the summer food and drinks. Once while I was lying out on a raft in the pool, Larry dove in for a swim. For a moment he forgot we were in public. He started kissing and sucking my toes and then working his way up and kissing my legs. Oh, the passion and the softness of my dirty little white boy! I even forgot for a moment and reached down to kiss him back; then we both suddenly realized that Agnes and Patrick were right there! We were so in love that we even had a hard time keeping our hands off one another around our spouses. I wore dark sunglasses so no one knew when I was watching Larry, and he did the same. We couldn't keep our eyes off each other, either. Well, we thought the kissing in the pool had gone unnoticed, but Joanne saw us. She smiled, and later she whispered, "So how long have you and my brother been in love?"

I smiled. "Long enough for us both to know we can't live without each other."

"Tonight after Agnes goes to bed, Larry and I can talk. I can't wait to tell Mom and Dad," Joanne said happily. "They'll be so glad to hear that he's finally leaving her! I'm so happy for the kids too! You'll make a good mom for them."

Later that night, Joanne and her brother had their talk about love and life. Larry was glad to share our love story. He had been saving money for the divorce, and I had been planning mine. It was all about timing. We wanted everything to be perfect for the kids. We had found a house and chosen a place where we were going to get married. It was one of the oldest buildings in town, built when President Lincoln was in office, and it was very charming. The house we decided to buy reminded him of home. It was an older home with built-in bookcases and love seats in the windows, a cozy fireplace, and big bedrooms for the kids. It also had a picket fence around the back and an oversized garage. We were getting close. Joanne was well pleased; it wasn't long before she was calling me regularly. She wanted to keep in touch and talk with her brother without Agnes finding out. It was happening. Soon we would be together.

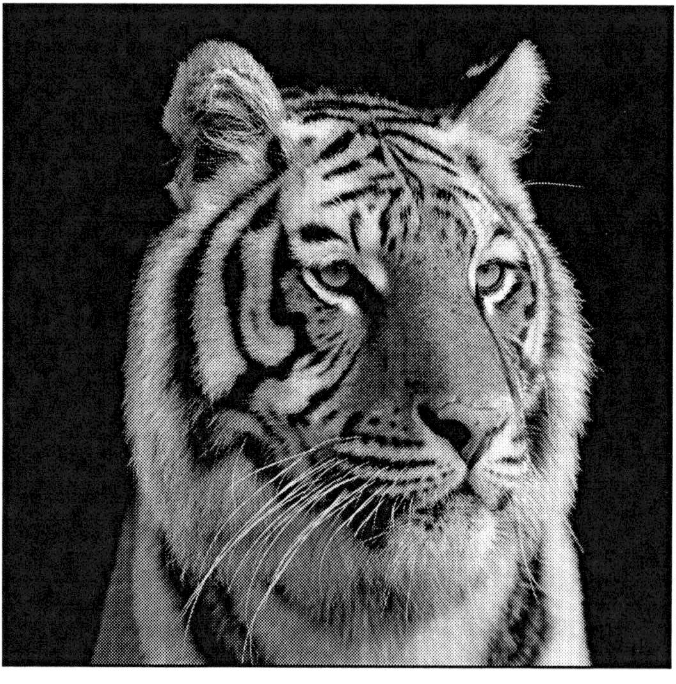

Chapter 16
Our Hairy Little Man

Larry and I had planned a four-day weekend together. Again he had sent Agnes away to her sister's, saying he had to play in a golf tournament. Patrick was out of town working and Levi wanted to spend time with his cousins. Everything was perfect. Our torrid love affair continued. We wanted to do something different, so we did. I had heard of a man down in the southern part of the state who owned tigers, lions, and bears. He even had three-week-old tiger cubs. I made a few calls, got directions, and we were off on an exciting adventure. We were going to hold and bottle-feed tiger cubs. I had dreamed of holding tiger cubs! Now, with Larry, another dream was about to come true.

When we arrived at the cat sanctuary, I couldn't believe my eyes! There were thirty-three big cats in all: tigers, lions, jaguars, and cougars. There were also big brown bears and bear cubs! I was so taken aback by what I was seeing out in the middle of nowhere that I didn't even hear Larry at first. "Laura! Look at that man!"

"What?" I said, too busy taking in all the beautiful animals.

"Laura, we're not getting out of this truck! Look!" he said while turning my head with his hands.

"Oh my God!" I said. There stood the most unusual looking human I'd ever seen. His head and face were covered with gray hair, and his beard was braided and hung past his knees. *Somewhere in there are eyes; I've just got to find them under all that gray hair.* "We have to get out, Larry; we've come so far! It'll be all right. Follow my lead." I reached for the door handle.

The man wore a blue bandana, and his hair was as long as his beard. He stood about four feet tall and weighed only about eighty pounds, hair and all. As I got closer I finally saw his eyes. They were blue, kind, and full of life. I reached out and shook his tiny hand, then yelled for Larry to come and meet Steve, the cat whisperer.

After introductions, Steve showed us his cats. They were magnificent! My favorite was the black jaguar. Later we sat down under a shade tree and fed the tiger cubs. It was wonderful. The kittens were tough and feral—nothing like I'd expected. I had scratches all over my legs, but I didn't care. It was nothing short of pure pleasure to enjoy those

Only the Heart Know's...

incredible animals. After a while, Steve brought out the bear cubs, and Larry enjoyed them even more than he had enjoyed the tiger cubs. He got to wrestle and roughhouse with them. Steve even played the guitar for us before we left, and he gave us one of his CDs. It was an experience I would never forget. On the way home, we enjoyed his funky music. Oh, what a day!

That evening Larry and I got all dressed up and went out to eat at a fine restaurant. We took our time, had cocktails and appetizers, and then ate a wonderful dinner. We held hands and stared into each other's eyes. We were very connected and in love.

Later that evening we drove out to the country, watched the sun set, and enjoyed a bottle of wine. Right around sunset, the deer came out with their young. We watched them graze on the tall green grass, and then we stayed there and made love over and over again. The warm breeze was blowing on our naked skin, the stars were in the sky with the moon—there were moments when I didn't know where I started and he began. I had never experienced lovemaking like ours; we were truly one. It was one of the happiest days of my life, and one I will never forget.

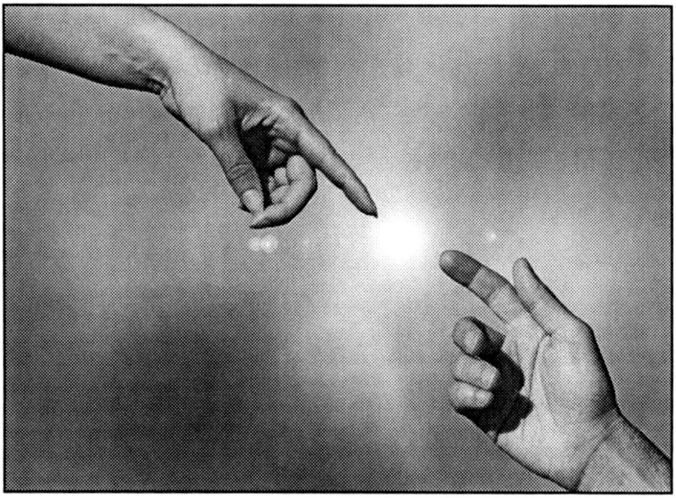

Chapter 17
Time To Move Forward

Larry and I were committed to each other. It was time to tell our spouses. Larry had saved some money and we had found our house. He had been searching out a good lawyer so Agnes couldn't "clean him out," as he said. My marriage wasn't as bad as Larry's. Patrick had his own issues. He was so caught up in his career, politics, and business that I don't think he ever even noticed I was pulling away. Being in the Vietnam War had changed him. He was emotionally shut down from all the death and the evil he had witnessed, and I thought I was entitled to more attention and love than Patrick could give me. I never stopped loving and caring about him, but it just wasn't working anymore. I wanted the fireworks and the butterflies. Larry wasn't a better man; he was just more interested in sharing himself with me. He was more available.

Summer had turned to fall and Larry had made plans to go on a mission with his church. They were going to build houses for poverty-stricken areas in New Orleans. He had mixed feelings about going. He didn't want to leave me. Our plan was to make our move toward the divorces when he got back from New Orleans. For some reason he wanted me to go first, but I didn't really understand why. After all, he was the one who was miserable. He had wanted out of his marriage years before I had wanted out of mine.

Larry leaving on the church mission was heart-rending for both of us. On the night before he left, he made up some excuse to stop by my house while Patrick was home. I was cleaning up from dinner and getting ready to give Levi a bath. While Larry was chatting with Patrick, he asked if I could go with him to pick out some supplies for his mission trip.

Oh my! I thought. But Patrick said, "Sure, take her. She'll be a great help!" Just like that I was in Larry's truck and we were together. Larry was rubbing my legs and kissing my hands.

He stopped at an empty church near the highway, then reached over and started kissing me, hugging me, and telling me how much he was going to miss me. "We'll never be apart again. I love you so much, sweetie!"

I told him I'd be waiting for him and missing him and that I loved him too. Then he asked me to make love to him. "Right here, in the church parking lot?"

Only the Heart Know's...

"Yes, Laura. God knows how much we love each other. It's all right. I won't see you for over a week. Please Laura, I need you so badly."

After a few moments, I let him have his way right there in front of God's house. *What's happening to me?* Somehow I was changing. I didn't know myself anymore. I was doing things with this man I never would have done before. He kept pushing me and I kept letting him. When I got home, I showered immediately. I felt empty and ashamed.

While Larry was away, I had some time to think. The phone calls all but stopped for a week. He still phoned, but only a few times, and he couldn't talk for long. I went through Larry-relationship withdrawal, but it was a good thing. I had time to think and catch my breath. I didn't like my reflection in the mirror. I seemed not to even know the person staring back at me. I felt I had lost myself. I needed some time alone. In my heart I knew I loved Larry and that he loved me, but when he got back there would have to be some changes. We both needed to get our divorces and get back to living truthful lives. I hated all the lies and sneaking around. They say the truth will set you free. I was ready to find out.

Life had turned into a true roller coaster ride—an adventure—while Larry was away. An old boyfriend emerged on the scene, only this guy was a great big handsome fish—a true catch, a dream come true, a Greek god. There was nothing average about this man—absolutely nothing.

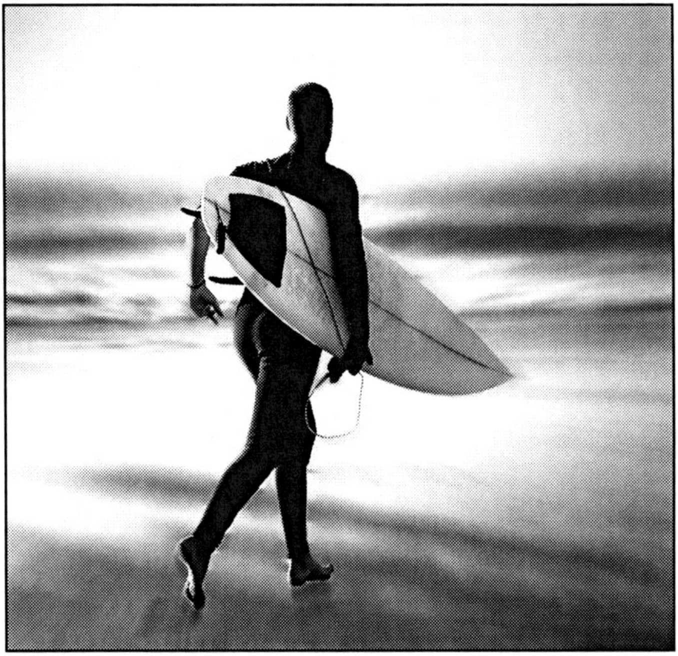

Chapter 18
The Greek God

Adam was only the best looking guy I'd ever seen or will ever see in my life. He stood six feet four inches tall and had beautiful blonde hair, crystal-blue eyes, and the stature of a bodybuilder. He was strong and cut to perfection. His hands were beautiful, slender, and long, and his voice was that of a trained vocalist—deep and debonair. His manners were exquisite, and he was lovely to chat with. To top it off, he was a doctor twice over. Adam was so accomplished that I knew I was with a divine human being when I was in his company. Walking into a room with him was simply amazing; everyone looked at this gorgeous man. He had very positive energy, and his presence demanded recognition. If Hitler were alive, he'd mess his pants over Adam. Yes, he was that perfect.

We first met in California. We were both young and chasing our dreams. I was walking on Laguna Beach in a snow-white sundress. I was tan, and my long, dark-brown hair was blowing in the wind. The sun was shining brightly, and the sand was soft and glistening. The waves were crashing hard on the shore. There were surfers everywhere, all of them trying to catch the perfect wave. That was when I saw him. *Oh my!* I couldn't take my eyes off him. He was exquisite, tall, and he looked so tan in contrast with his blonde hair. *That face and those eyes! Hmm.* I just hoped he would notice me. I also remember thinking, *I hope he isn't gay*. I kept walking, and suddenly there he was, walking next to me.

"Beautiful day for the beach," he said.

"Yes, it is," I said.

"Mind if I walk with you?"

That's how our relationship began, and we spent the next few days together. We were both young and free, and we enjoyed each other immensely. We had time and learned to care for one another deeply. Maybe we even loved each other. Our paths just went different directions.

Eventually I moved from California back to the Midwest. Adam had become a doctor and moved out of the country. Later he wanted to be a surgeon, and he had gone back to school to do just that. He had tried to walk up the aisle twice to get married, but each time he backed out at the last minute. He said they were both beautiful women who were very successful, but he always saw my face when he thought of marrying. So here he was again, near my little town, and he wanted to see me. He wanted either closure or to find out whether we were destined to be together.

I have to admit that Adam and I had corresponded a few times on the Internet. We also had made a few mutual friends through the years, and sometimes we would try to keep up with one another through them. But I didn't expect to see him again, let alone hear that he needed closure regarding our past relationship. Now I had to wonder whether God was playing a trick on me or whether, perhaps, this was divine interference. Was he trying to save me from attaching myself to the most average man alive—one who was married and had children; one who was not too bright and had a full-figured wife with lots of issues? *Hmm, okay ... I'm still married to Patrick—not happily, but still married just the same. Well, let's just see what Adam has to say.* I wanted to know whether he could give me butterflies and fireworks like Larry did. If he did, Larry would be out, plain and simple. Adam didn't have the baggage that Larry had. Besides, I used to really like and respect this guy. Oh, what a man!

Adam and I met near my home at a little college town. If it was possible after ten years, he was even better looking than I remembered. He was very kind and considerate. I had to reach up to give him a hug. I had forgotten how tall six feet four inches was, especially after being with my dirty little white boy. I was beginning to remember the high standards I'd always put on my friends and on those I dated. I was home again—in my own realm. In a lot of ways Adam was like Patrick—a real man. Adam treated me like a lady. He never implied anything disrespectful. Being a good Christian, unlike me, he would never do anything that would jeopardize another's integrity, nor would he ask anyone else to do any such thing. He wanted me to know how he felt, and he said he would wait … for a while. He said that he would give me some time to decide and that I would have to leave Patrick if I chose to be with him. He never told me it was going to be easy or that we would live in a rose garden. He just wanted to spend the rest of his life with Levi and me.

I told him I could never give him children, but he said that was all right too. He said if I were willing to let him love my son and give him the opportunity to be a father, he would share the responsibility with Patrick. It would all work out. My God, what honesty and wholesomeness! That's the kind of man Adam was. Adam would stay in town for six weeks. He had to study and get ready for another internship. In the meantime, I would think it over and let him know what I wanted to do.

Chapter 19
Choices

Three different men, three different choices. What's a middle-aged woman to do? I was truly lost. The only man I was sure about was Levi. I loved him with all my heart. But when he was all grown up, what would I want? Whom would I love? Who would love me? Patrick, who was a good provider, the father of my son, and my husband, was emotionally unavailable. Larry, who was wild, unpredictable, and average, swore his undying love for me. And Adam, who was a god and embodied absolute perfection, wanted to share his glorious life with me. I was very confused.

With Larry gone I was thinking more clearly. I certainly didn't have my head in the clouds. I had landed on my feet and was completely grounded. He'd be back in a few days, and I was anxious to see him even though I thought I'd try to put him off for a few extra days. I needed to be strong so I could be straight with him, and I hoped he would be straight with me. As for Patrick, I would try to pull some attention and love out of him so I could make the best decision for all of us. I wanted to know how he really felt about our life and us. Maybe he'd already thrown in the towel. He might want to just work and live a quiet life, with the exception of being with his son. I was at the crossroads of my life, and I didn't know which one to choose.

Chapter 20
Larry's Homecoming

Larry was home from his mission trip. On Monday morning the phone calls began again. It was funny; I wanted to see him and talk to him but I was also sick to my stomach and shaky because I wanted to get out of this situation.. I finally took his call. "Hello?"

"Well, hello sweetie! How are you? I missed you so much! I love you dearly, Laura. Can I see you today? We can meet at the apartment. I have all kinds of presents I picked up for you while I was away," he said with a giggle. "One is *very* special to me. I want you to wear it for me."

"Oh, Larry, you didn't have to do that. I want to know all about your trip."

He sounded confused. "You *are* going to meet me today, aren't you?"

"Hmm … no, I can't … .I'm sorry. I have a meeting today at noon about the upcoming fundraiser, and I'm going to Dorothy's tonight to meet friends for dinner. I'm really sorry."

"Laura, what's wrong?"

"Nothing, I'm just busy," I said softly. "Larry, in a few days we need to talk. I want you to think about what you really want out of life, and then we can talk."

"Talk?" He sounded angry. "Talk about what?"

"Us ... about us, Larry. I've been thinking ... I can't go on like this anymore. I love you, Larry, but I'm starting to feel awful about all the sneaking around and lying. I want the whole world to know how much we love one another. I want to be proud of our love, not hide it in an apartment or a hotel room. Do you understand?"

"Yes, I do. I feel the same way. I love you with all my heart. I don't want to lose you. I've just been planning and saving my money."

"Okay, just take a few days and be sure ... then we can talk," I said as kindly as I could.

"Laura, what's happened? I love you, sweetie." He sounded pitiful. "Please ... please, Laura ... we can work this out. I can't live without you."

"Don't worry, Larry. Everything is fine." *I need to start him thinking about something else.* "I can't wait to see my gifts! I'll bet you've been a naughty boy. What did you buy me? More lingerie? The really sexy kind?"

"Yeah … that, some jewelry, and a book," he said, laughing.

"Okay … well, I'm looking forward to it! Talk with you soon."

"Okay … guess I'll call you later. I love you, sweetie."

Later that afternoon I headed to Dorothy's house. She lived in the same little college town where I met Adam. We were all friends: Adam, Dorothy, and I. Walking into Dorothy's home was like stepping back in time. She owned an old Victorian house with an English flower garden, and it was filled with antiques. She had never been married and owned four lovely cats, two dogs, and lots of fish that she kept in her pond. I had given one of her cats, Betty, to her over ten years ago. Dorothy was the sister I never had. I loved her. She was good and kind and understanding. We had been friends for almost twenty years.

Of course she knew Adam was in town, and she knew about Larry. The problem was that she was a friend of Kathryn, the flight attendant who used to date Larry, as was I. I had a funny feeling she was trying to tell me something about Larry and Kathryn. She was very uneasy every time I spoke about Larry. She kept reminding me of how wonderful Adam was and she kept saying she didn't trust Larry. I told her she didn't know Larry and that if she met him maybe she would feel different about him.

"I don't know," she said. "I think he's a snake in the grass."

I wondered why she thought that. There had to be a reason.

It wasn't long before all our friends gathered at Dorothy's beautiful house. We were all outside enjoying the waterfall in her pond and watching the hummingbirds and butterflies flitting around her many flowers. We were drinking red wine and catching up with all the latest gossip in all our lives. Dorothy stepped out with a cheese-and-fruit tray and a couple more bottles of wine. We were really enjoying ourselves.

Then my cell phone rang. "Oh, it's only my son," I said, excusing myself to answer my phone. But it wasn't; it was Larry.

"Where does Dorothy live?" he asked.

"Why?"

"I'm in the area and I thought I'd drop by to say hi."

"I don't think that's a good idea, Larry."

"Laura, it's okay. I've got all evening. I told Agnes I was going to Hooters with some of the guys at work. Bob's birthday, you know? Besides, I really want to see you."

"All right … she lives on Queens Street. You'll see my car."

Only the Heart Know's...

"I'll be there in just a few minutes, sweetie. Goodbye."
What am I going to tell Dorothy?

Larry came and I introduced him to all my friends. Everyone seemed to like him—it was because of all that charisma and charm. We couldn't help but hold hands and kiss a little. The wine and the sound of the waterfall really relaxed all of us. Every time I looked at Larry, he was staring at me. It seemed he could look right down to my very soul. I was trying to take it all in.

I stepped into the house for a moment to go to the bathroom, and Dorothy followed me in. "Laura?" she called out.

"I'm in here—in the bathroom. I'll be right out," I said.

As I stepped out of the bathroom, she met me. "Laura, I know you didn't know this, but Kathryn might be stopping by. What if she gets here and you're here with Larry?" she asked.

"What? I don't know what you're talking about." I said.

She began wringing her hands. "I ... I don't want to tell you this, but he's been seeing her too. He even told her dad he was leaving Agnes and was going to take care of Kathryn for the rest of her life. She believes *she* will be the next Mrs. Williams. That's what Larry's told her, or led her to believe. I guess he's been telling her she'll be the first one he calls after the divorce. I'm sorry. I've wanted to tell you. He's just a snake. Laura, I'm so sorry," she said with humility.

"What? I don't believe you! He told me it was over between them! No! No, you're wrong! He *loves* me! I *know* he does!" I was in the midst of denial.

I all but staggered back to the cocktail party on the patio. I sat for a few minutes while watching and listening to Larry talk to the guys. *How could he do this to me?* I thought. Then I excused myself, telling everyone that I had to get home because my sitter was having trouble getting Levi to bed.

Larry followed me out to my car. "Would you like to get a hotel room for a few hours? I have this amazing nightgown I've bought for you. I'd love to rip it off and then devour you!" he said with a laugh.

"No, not tonight Larry. I really have to go home. I'm sorry you've wasted an evening of freedom. Maybe if you hang out for a while, Kathryn will show up. If you're lucky, maybe *she'll* wear that hot little number for you." I slammed my door.

His eyes got as big as quarters. "What? What did you say?"

"You heard me, you son of a bitch!" I shouted.

Only the Heart Know's...

He ran to his truck and followed me home.

He kept flashing his headlights to get me to stop. He kept calling my cell phone. We were becoming dangerous to other and ourselves on the roads, so I stopped next to a cornfield. Larry got out of his truck and walked over to my car. "What in the hell is going on, Laura?" he shouted.

"Dorothy told me about you and Kathryn. I thought it was over between you two! That's what you *told* me, Larry." I began sobbing.

"Oh baby … it is! She just won't let go. She's in love with me. After her father died, I felt obligated to help her through a hard time. That's all, Laura. I'm really in love with you. You have to *know* that. You and I are magical together. This thing with Kathryn … I'm just letting her down easy. Please stop crying. Let me hold you, sweetie. Everything's going to be all right. I promise, Baby." He said it all so softly and convincingly.

Well, I fell for his song and dance. I'm sure I needed to. To think otherwise would have made him a monster. We sat there for a few hours and made up. We talked about his trip, and he put a silver bracelet on my wrist. He asked me to never take it off. I knew I was in over my head. This guy was *good*, and I was addicted to him mentally and physically. I was in real trouble for the first time in my life.

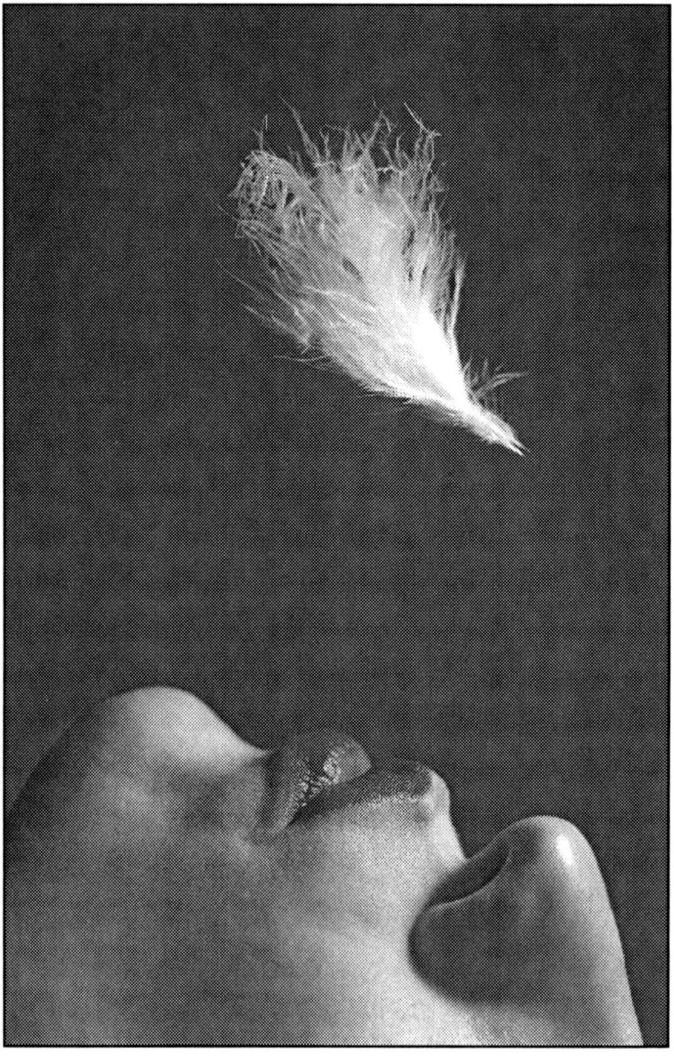

Chapter 21
Dorothy's Secret and Truth

I needed to meet Larry on neutral ground to talk about our future, so I phoned Dorothy and asked if I could meet Larry at her house. She agreed. She wanted something to be worked out for her friends—Kathryn and me. She didn't like Larry at all, and she had her reasons. She didn't like what he had done to two of her best friends with his lying and deception. So after talking, we decided Larry and I would meet at her house.

Larry got there a lot earlier than I. That's when Dorothy had her talk with him. She asked him straight out which one of her friends he loved and what in the hell he was doing hurting two wonderful women the way he had. She held nothing back. He answered her the only way he knew how. Charmingly and convincingly, he told her he was in love with me. He said that he was sorry for hurting Kathryn and that he really wanted to spend the rest of his life with me.

That's when Dorothy played her trump card. "And your wife? What about her?" she asked.

"I'm leaving her, of course ... after Laura leaves Patrick."

"What?" she said. "*You're* the one with the miserable wife! And those are your words, Larry, not mine," she reminded him. "And you're the one who's wanted out of your marriage for years! Oh, and the way you have strung Kathryn along makes me sick! And just why in the hell does Laura have to leave Patrick first? What are you, scared?"

That's when Larry excused himself to go to the restroom. I'm sure he was getting very uncomfortable with the conversation. But within a few minutes, he came back to the kitchen table naked as a jaybird with the exception of his gray boxers! Dorothy was busy making another kettle of hot tea when she turned and saw him standing there.

She couldn't believe her eyes! "What are you doing?" she asked, almost laughing at the sight of him.

He grinned. "Well, do you want to make love or have great sex? Maybe when Laura gets here we could all have a threesome, what with you two being such good friends and everything."

"What the hell! You're such a dirty little snake!" she yelled.

Larry began chasing her down the hall and around her bed. "Oh, come on! You know you want me. I'm sure Laura's told you how wonderful I am," he said, grinning.

"Larry, I said no! Stop right now! Laura will be here soon! Stop chasing me and get your clothes on! Right now, damn it! I can't stand the sight of you!"

He finally relented. "Okay, if that's how you feel about it. I thought you two girls would jump on the chance to have a threesome with me," he said cockily.

"Larry, I hate to tell you this; I mean, you should already know it; Laura's not that kind of girl," she said proudly.

"She may not have been, but I bet she would have a threesome for me," he said arrogantly. "See Dorothy, Laura loves me unconditionally. She'd do just about anything for me. And by the way, I wouldn't tell her what happened here, okay?"

That's about when I pulled up in the driveway and honked my horn.

"Hi Dorothy," I said, and then I gave Larry a kiss. "Hello Larry. How are my two best friends?"

Dorothy excused herself. She said she had shopping to do and a friend to meet for lunch. She looked frazzled. "You guys take your time and get everything worked out one way or another. Laura, I'll talk to you later," she said as she walked out of her yard. She never looked back.

Hmm, what's wrong with her? I thought.

Larry and I walked into her house and sat down at the kitchen table. I could see that they had been drinking hot tea. The kettle was still warm, so I poured myself some hot water and made a cup of Earl Grey. It smelled great. Larry was sitting there drinking his tea and watching me. I looked at him. "So, what's going on?"

"Oh nothing. We were waiting for you," he said without expression.

I nodded. "Well, I think we need to have a serious talk. The fact is, I don't think you will ever leave Agnes. I know you say you can't stand her and that you were never in love with her, but I don't know … I can feel it in my gut. Maybe it's the kids, or the money … I think you really love me but—"

"Laura, you couldn't be more wrong! I've saved over fourteen thousand dollars for us. I'll show it to you. It's at home in my secret hiding spot. I've spoken with a friend who just went through a divorce, and he couldn't be happier. I love you dearly, Laura. Please give me a little more time." Then his tone of voice and facial expression changed drastically. "And what about you? When are you leaving Patrick? Why should I have to go first?"

"Larry, I'm really confused. I know in my heart without question that you love me ... but I don't know anymore ... I don't like what I've become ... the other woman. It's not me. I need to feel safe in a relationship; secure. I want the whole world to know how I feel about you. Life is about sharing and evolving into a better person. I have never loved someone as much as I love you and felt loved so little all at the same time. Confusing, isn't it? And, well ... an old boyfriend of mine has recently contacted me. He says he needs closure, so lately I've been thinking about you, him, and Patrick, and honestly, I don't know what I want."

Larry got up from his chair and wrapped his arms around me. "Laura, it's me you want. We belong together, now and forever," he whispered. "I will never leave you again," he said while unbuttoning my shirt. "I've never made love in a hundred-year-old bed with goose-down pillows." he said softly. A few moments later we were in Dorothy's guest room making passionate love to one another. I loved all his kissing and caressing. He was *so damn good* at making love. It was like going to the moon and back again. Larry had cast his spell, and I was stuck up in the clouds, drifting.

Larry kissed me goodbye and left to get back to work. He all but skipped down the sidewalk and through the gate to his truck. He was really happy. He said his life had really just begun. We had decided to get our divorces and work everything out. I stayed behind and cleaned up the guest room, and then took a quick shower.

It was not long before Dorothy came home. She walked into the kitchen and set her few shopping bags on the table. "Oh, hello! What did you buy?" I asked her as I was still happy and glowing from thinking about Larry.

"I got a new purse," she said in a quiet voice.

"What's wrong, Dorothy?"

She slowly looked up at me. "Do you really love him, Laura?"

"Oh my God, yes! With all my heart! I can't explain it, Dorothy; I just light up when he's around. I've never felt this way about anyone before and … well, I can't explain this feeling to you. You have to feel it for yourself. This is a once-in-a-lifetime love."

Then I noticed Dorothy wasn't looking at me. She was looking away, deep in thought. "What did you work out?" she asked somberly.

"Oh! We're going to work *everything* out! He loves me, Dorothy! I can't wait! He says our lives have just begun. We might even have someone—maybe his sister—be a surrogate mother for us so we can have our own children," I said happily. "Our lives have just begun."

Dorothy smiled. "I hope you're right, Laura. Please be careful. I don't like him. I can't explain it, but ... I just don't trust him." She seemed distant.

She'll change her mind. She just needs to get to know him better.

CHAPTER 22
Adam Says Farewell

Dorothy was so mad at Larry that she decided to call Adam back into the picture. *I'll stop Larry dead in his tracks*, she thought. No one could compete with Adam. With one phone call, Dorothy had Adam's attention. She invited him back for another visit, only this time she urged him to completely tell Laura how he felt about her. *Maybe this will keep her away from Larry so she can find some real happiness*, she thought. *After all who could say no to the most perfect man alive?* Adam agreed to come, but he did so for a different reason—a long farewell.

A few weeks later, there was a quiet little knock at Laura's front door. Moonlight and Polly were barking and letting everyone know someone was there. I thought it was one of the neighborhood kids coming over to join the other kids for a swim. Much to my surprise, there stood my Greek god! "Oh my God! How are you? Come in, Adam," I said.

"Hello Laura, how are you?" he asked. "Can we talk somewhere? I have something I have to tell you."

"Sure, let's go out on the porch swing where I can watch the kids swim and we can visit. Can I get you something to drink?" I asked. We both settled down with some iced tea and began to talk. It was not long before all the kids came over to meet Adam. I told Levi that he was an old friend who was passing through and had stopped to say hello. The boys were impressed with the way he looked. He was very strong and musclebound. They all thought he was some kind of superman. Adam enjoyed all the attention, and it wasn't long before the kids were back to swimming and playing.

"You see Laura, I've been called back to military duty. They need doctors. I will be leaving for the Middle East soon," he said. "I'm not sure of all the details yet, but I think I'll be away for at least a year. Laura, you know how much I love you and will always love you, but I have to go on with my life. You haven't left Patrick, and I've been waiting and praying for someone to share my life with. I met someone—another doctor. We met at a Bible-study class, and I think I'm in love with her. We work together, and I need to release you and myself from anything more

Only the Heart Know's...

for now. I need to give this a chance—myself a chance—for some love and happiness."

I understood completely. "Adam, you go and live your life to the fullest. I will always love you too. Maybe someday we will find each other again. You are such a good man," I said, looking down. I was thinking to myself, *How could you let this kind man leave your life?*

"Laura, if things don't work out, I'll look you up when I return. Maybe you will be free, and who knows?" he said.

"Yeah, who knows?"

She will marry him, and quick! I'm sure of it! I thought to myself. *How could I be so foolish?* We sat there on the swing and watched Levi and the kids play. Adam adored Levi. He thought he was a handsome and good boy. We talked about the weather, the war, and of course our friend Dorothy. It wasn't long before he said he had to go. I walked him to the car, and with a big hug and a small kiss on the cheek, he was gone—out of my life once again. I then thought to myself, *I'm left with an angry man and an average man. I let the best slip from my grasp.*

CHAPTER 23
Rolling In Money

The next hot, sunny day, I was enjoying a sunbath and reading a good book about Princess Diana. It had been written by her butler and was fascinating. I enjoyed a commoner's point of view—the viewpoint of someone who was close to the princess. She was the most photographed woman in the world, and she was beautiful. Her story was heartbreaking. She loved Princes Charles, but her fairytale life was anything but a fairy tale. It was more like a nightmare.

As I read about her, I remembered where I'd been when the news of her sudden and unexpected death broke on the news. I had been in Texas with my husband and my baby son visiting family and friends during the Labor Day weekend. I sat in shock as we watched the news broadcast telling of her untimely death. I also remembered watching her when I was seventeen when she was marrying Prince

Charles. She was lovely! I thought she was the luckiest woman in the world. Now she was dead in a car crash with her lover. She didn't deserve to have her life end in that way. And she'd left behind two boys whom she had loved dearly.

As I read, I thought of the time when I was in a department store getting my first bra—a training bra with a little pink bow on it. I was in line with my grandmother to purchase my coming-of-age bra when the news of Elvis's untimely death was broadcast over the loudspeaker. Everyone stopped. The ladies around us started crying. The King was dead. Buying a first training bra was hard enough for a thirteen-year-old girl, but to have Elvis die while doing it—tragic.

I was beginning to get hot, and I was getting up to take a swim when I heard Larry's oh-so-familiar whistle. "What ya doing?" he asked, grinning.

"Oh, just reading and getting a little sun. What are you doing home in the middle of the day?"

"I came to see you. I wanted to show you something. Put on your cover-up and come home with me."

"Okay, but where's Agnes?" I asked.

He smiled. "She's at work. Come on, sweetie. I want to spend some time with you."

We walked over to his house and went upstairs to the in-laws' quarters. He was proud of the upstairs because he had done most of the work himself. He sat me down on the bed. He seemed so excited! He went to the closet, reached into the wall, and pulled out a coffee can. He brought it over to me and asked me to open it. I did, and there I found over fourteen thousand dollars that he had stashed away from his greedy, selfish wife.

He looked at me. "Do you believe me now? I told you I was saving so we could be together. I love you so much, Laura!

We laughed and giggled like two children. We laid the money all over the bed and made love for hours among the bills. We were so happy!

Afterwards I tried to take a quick shower, but he followed me and we made love again. He couldn't get enough.

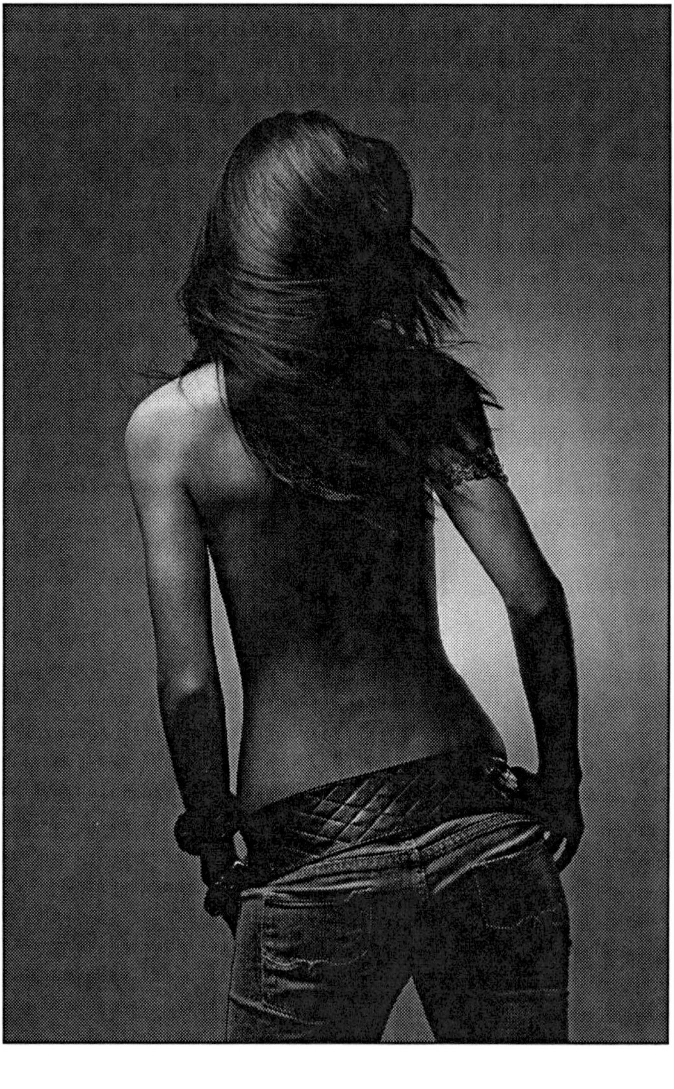

Chapter 24
Larry Is Caught in the Act

Late one evening I was again taking a midnight skinny dip. There's something very relaxing about swimming under the stars and the moon. I slept better after a relaxing swim. I slept even better after a moonlit lovemaking session. So I swam and listened to my soft music, but I mostly listened for Larry's familiar whistle. I really wanted him that particular evening. But my desire was to no avail; he didn't show. I swam and swam, trying to get all the sexual energy out.

Larry sat out on his back porch, smoking a cigarette. He could hear me swimming. He could also hear my music playing. He looked up at the sky and saw the sparkling stars and the moon. He thought, *Why won't that bitch just go to bed? But no. She's got to be on the computer. EBay's ruining my evening with Laura. God, I need her tonight. If I can't be with her, I'll just listen to her swim and dream of her making love to me.*

He finished his cigarette, undid his khaki shorts, and pulled out his penis. In his mind, he was with me in the pool, our lips kissing, our bodies moving as one, the warm water swirling around us. He masturbated to the beat of my music. It was easy for him to be there in his mind, but just when he was ready to climax, Agnes walked out on the porch and caught him with his back arched and his head lying back. "What are you *doing?*" she yelled.

He looked down and saw that he was coming in his hand. *Back to reality*, he thought.

Agnes walked back into the house, disgusted.

The next morning, Larry couldn't wait to tell me what had happened. I was driving Levi to school, and Larry was stopped at the corner gas station. I saw him and he motioned for me to stop. "Can you have a cup of coffee with me after you drop off Levi?"

"Sure, I'll meet you at the coffee shop in a few minutes." Then I was off to take Levi to school.

"What does Mr. Williams want to talk to you about, Mama?" Levi asked.

"Oh, I'm sure it has something to do with tutoring his son." I felt awful about lying once again. *I don't know how much longer I can keep this up.*

Only the Heart Know's...

After dropping off Levi, I headed straight for the coffee shop. Larry was waiting for me. He had already gotten our coffee. "Let's talk out in my truck," he said.

In his truck, he explained everything that had happened the night before, and I started laughing. "Why Larry, I didn't know you had to do things like that!" I giggled.

"It's not funny, Laura. She was a maniac last night after she caught me. She put me through hell!"

"Well, I guess you shouldn't jack off if you think you might get caught." I laughed again. "Besides, you shouldn't need to jack off. We make love all the time," I said, still grinning.

"I know … I just couldn't help myself. I mean, there you were … so close. I could see you, I could hear you, and I wanted you! That nasty bitch just wouldn't go to bed," he said.

"Larry, don't talk about her that way. Just get a divorce. Then we can be together and these things won't happen. Besides, I'd like to watch you jack off," I said, joking.

He nodded. "You're right. Well, I'd better get to work. I just wanted you to know why I didn't come over last night. I wanted to," he said.

"It's okay. We have plenty of time," I said while getting out of the truck.

He looked at me through the window. "Laura, I love you, sweetie, with all my heart."

I nodded. "I know; I love you too."

Chapter 25
Two Lives

Somewhere I read that sometimes we have to be willing to get rid of the life we planned so we can have the true life that is waiting for us. I hope whoever wrote that is right. I was getting ready to embark on a life that was completely unexpected, all for love.

Fall quickly turned to winter and Christmas was coming, ready or not. Larry and I had decided that after the holidays we would make our move. We spent as much time together as we could. We often met to go Christmas shopping for the kids and for each other. As we were shopping, we came across the most beautiful Christmas tree. It was entirely pink. Mary Kay would have been proud! We both wanted it instantly! It was completely different from what we'd had with our spouses. Larry said he would run out and buy it for us the day after Christmas for next year. He could store it at work until we got our house. There was so much magic and excitement! We were planning for our family and the future.

I had decided to cancel my annual Christmas Eve party for several reasons. First, Larry and I didn't want to go through hiding our feelings anymore. Second, I didn't feel like celebrating after what had happened the year before with grandma's death. But mainly Larry and I really wanted to be together. We were both ready to shed our old lives and begin anew. We were both hoping by the New Year that we would be free to live our lives together and love each other openly.

Larry and I celebrated Christmas a few days before Christmas. I was overwhelmed by all his gifts! He filled my car from floor to ceiling! If I had known what he was planning I would've bought stock at Victoria Secret! He said he could never buy sexy things for Agnes. He said, "She's entirely too big." He laughed. "She'd look ridiculous! Just the other day, she was bending over to pick up laundry, and she was naked. I thought I'd puke right there! I had to cover my eyes."

"Oh Larry, I wish you wouldn't tell me such things. It's far too much information." I said, laughing. But I was thinking, *How sad.*

Christmas and New Year's came and went, and Larry still had not made his move. Night after night he kept telling me he would tell her that he wasn't in love with her and that he wanted a divorce and that he would then move out. He said that I could follow suit soon afterward. I think he was afraid of Agnes. I tried to be supportive and wait. That's all I could do.

I kept reassuring him that we had a wonderful life waiting for us and that all the dreams he had shared with me could come true. He just had to believe in himself and us. Together, anything was possible. He seemed to love me more and more, but I had a bad feeling about things. He was terrified of Agnes and of losing his kids and of losing what he valued most—money, the one thing that doesn't last. He didn't like the fact that she would get half of what he earned. I was afraid he was about to come face-to-face with greed and that he would lose. He wasn't that strong in character.

I was ready to move on, and I was just waiting on Larry, but all he wanted to do was make love whenever we could. He said it gave him the strength to face "Fat Ass" every evening.

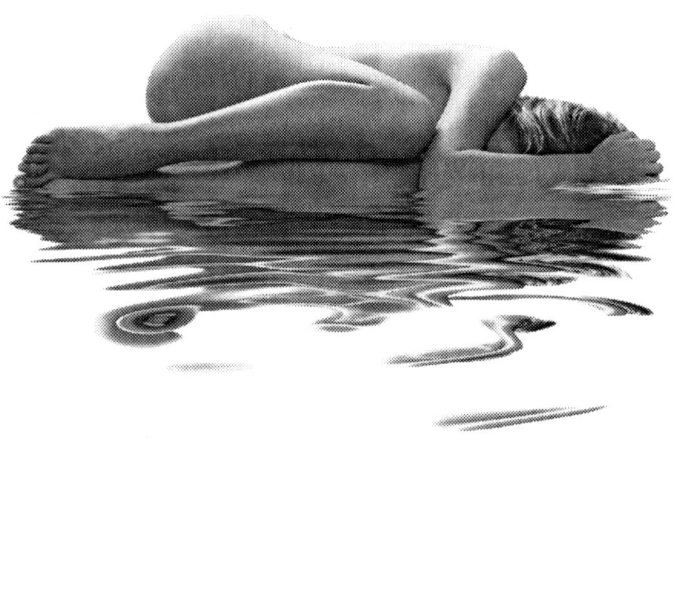

Chapter 26
The Warmth of Loves ... the Coldness of Betrayal

After all Larry's promises and planning, I thought that we'd be on our way to a bright, beautiful future. He sure could talk and dream, make love, and make me laugh and giggle. But anything more permanent seemed to be hard for him. I started wondering whether my friends were right about him. Dorothy and Jessie kept warning me that something wasn't right—that *Larry* wasn't right. But despite their warnings that he was nothing short of pure evil, I waited for him. I was in a fog—the fog of denial.

He'd said he loved me and we'd shopped for a new home and furniture. We'd talked and planned about how our simple wedding would be. We had also decided how we were going to tell the kids and merge the family into one. I was completely sincere in all my actions with Larry. He had convinced me that he was the man I was supposed to spend the rest of my life with. I have to admit that in the beginning, I was careful and only amused by his attentions. I never thought I'd fall in love with this plain, average man. But the warmth of his love was turning cold. The pain of knowing what his intentions were was beginning to take hold of my very soul. It was ugly and dark. I was at the start of a spiral heading down to the depths of hell, and I was all alone.

Depression is a horrible state of mind, especially when your actions are the reason you're there. I had been really awful. Now the guilt of my love affair was taking a toll. I knew in my heart that Larry loved me, and I'm sure if he'd been a man of better character we could have been very happy together. But he wasn't a man of his word. His behavior was entirely different from his promises. I know that if I'd been willing, we'd have been meeting at hotels and apartments for years. But to give up half of his assets? He'd never do that. I knew deep in my heart it would be much easier for him to replace me and stay married to a woman he didn't love. I just kept hoping he'd stand up for our love and be a good, strong man. I had banked on it mentally and emotionally. I was also praying that God would work all this out for me.

After another wonderful, pleasurable afternoon with Larry, we decided to go shopping again. This time we headed for the pet store. We happily picked out a puppy that he wanted for our new family. He hated the pugapoo Agnes had bought last summer. Larry kept telling me that one day he was going to load that stupid dog up in his truck and dump it off someplace where it couldn't find its way back home. I felt sorry for poor Stanley. Larry felt more than hatred for that dog. It gave me chills. He said that after work he would go home and pick up his daughter, Elizabeth, and then go back to the pet store and buy the part-lab mixed breed we'd picked out. He was so excited he could hardly wait.

After a long goodbye, I headed home. I told Larry to bring the puppy over after he bought her so we would name her together. He gladly agreed. Larry was almost too happy. It was nice to see him that way.

Later that evening, I was cleaning up from dinner when Patrick made known his intention to make love that evening. I was in a sheer panic. I had just spent the afternoon with Larry. There was no way I could make love with Patrick—I'm just not made that way—so I started drinking a little wine. It wasn't long before a little glass of wine turned into a whole bottle. I thought if I just went to sleep he'd leave me alone. Then here came Larry and Elizabeth with the new puppy; only it wasn't the puppy we'd picked out. It was another little foo-foo dog. I couldn't believe my eyes!

"What this?" I asked when I opened the back door.

"My new puppy!" Elizabeth announced.

"I see that, honey. You're a very lucky little girl," I said.

I was really starting to feel the effects of the wine, and I was visually annoyed and disturbed by Larry's choice. I could tell he really hadn't wanted to buy that dog. I think he did it out of guilt. And I was still faced with dealing with Patrick. I was not happy.

After Elizabeth and Larry left with their new dog, I started drinking rum. I really tied one on. Then I took a few too many sleeping pills. I wanted out of my awful dilemma. I couldn't face Patrick, and I was feeling abandoned by Larry. *How can he let this keep going on? Why doesn't he do something? I can't go on like this.* Well, it wasn't long before the alcohol and pills set in. I knew there was no turning back, so I thought I'd just see this ride through until the end—whatever that end was.

I landed myself right in the hospital. Now I was in real hell. When I awoke I was cold and frightened. I could feel a freezing cotton sheet next to my skin, and I suddenly realized I was in so much pain from this little average man that I couldn't go on living a lie. I deserved more. The anguish of what I had done and what I had been doing was staring me in the face. The monster was real, and the monster was me.

It was time for change. I recall having to spend time in therapy. I also had to go on medication to help me with my depression and to get the courage to face life. Of course Larry didn't want me telling my doctors about him and the affair, but I did anyway.

During my time in therapy, my doctor told me I was dealing with a psychopath, or at the very least a sociopath. Either way, Larry was not going to be easy for me to deal with, especially since he still had his hold on me. I was going to really try to see him with different eyes—truthful eyes. I wanted to see him the way Dorothy and Jessie saw him. Or did I?

Chapter 27
The Fundraising Dinner

Around the end of January, I had a big fundraising dinner planed for our new library. I had worked hard with the library committee to make the dinner a success. I had worked on the official poster and the golden tickets, which were to sell at a hundred dollars apiece. Then I met with the local newspaper for a press release. I sold lots of tickets. It seemed that everybody who was somebody in town would attend. It was going to be great fun—a very festive time. We wanted the dinner to be alive with music and colorful beads like Mardi Gras in New Orleans. With grownups playing like children, it was going to be the kickoff celebration of the year!

    I had told Larry I'd like that evening to be our coming-out night. I thought that would give him a few extra weeks to get himself together and give him a timeline to work toward. He seemed really happy about that decision; he couldn't wait until the dinner. He said that he was proud of the work I had done and that he wanted to be a part of it. Every time we met at the apartment or at a hotel, he would make mad, passionate love to me. He would hold me for hours. We would lie in our nest and dream about our bright future. He would call me the new and improved Mrs. Williams. But to me he was always my dirty little white boy.

The day of my fundraising dinner finally came. Larry still hadn't left Agnes. I was disappointed, but too busy working and planning to really focus on the issue. Larry had phoned me several times at work that day. I was busy working with the kindergarten class, and his phone calls were interrupting my work. He was exhausting me. He kept telling me over and over again how much he loved me and how much I meant to him. Finally, the principal came downstairs to my class and asked why I was getting so many phone calls at work. He said I would have to accept them after school was out. I agreed. Larry had gone too far. He was acting strangely. This, of all nights, was not the night to be as needy as he was being.

I thought he was just acting out and feeling guilty for not being able to be with me that night at the dinner, but I was past it; I just wanted the dinner to be a great success.

Only the Heart Know's...

Larry and all his needs were going to have to wait. After school I had three messages asking me to phone him, so on my way home I gave him a quick call.

"Hello?" he said.

"Hi there. So what's so important that you have to call me so many times?"

"I just wanted you to know how much I love you and that nothing will ever change that, Laura," he said somberly.

"I know. Listen, I'll call you tomorrow when this dinner is over, okay?"

"Okay. Laura, I will always love you." He hung up.

Well, he is acting strange, I thought. *But I can't worry about that now. I have to get myself ready and happy for my dinner. I'll run home, take a quick bath, change, and meet with my hairdresser. Then it's party time—for the big kids, that is!*

When I got home, Patrick and Levi had their boys' night out planned—pizza and a war movie. I glanced at the mail and listened to my messages. The fundraising dinner was a sellout! I was happy and nervous all at the same time. Oh, what a night! I headed down the hall to my bathroom to run my bath. I poured in some lavender and baby oil to calm me down a little. I was getting ready to slip into my robe when I thought of something I needed to tell my husband. I was walking back down the hallway when I ran into Agnes. She'd just walked into my house!

"What are you doing here?" I said, feeling startled.

"Laura, I know about you and Larry!" she shrieked. "Do you want to do this here in front of your son and husband, or do you want to take it outside?"

"Outside," I said firmly. "Patrick, could you please turn off my bath water? I'm stepping out to talk to Agnes. I'll be right back." I closed the front door behind me.

Agnes handed me a letter—a poorly written letter at that. It stated that Larry had been having an affair.

Agnes looked at me. "I just want to know if it's you."

I nodded. "Yes, it's me. But you have to believe me, Agnes, I'm sorry you had to find out this way."

Her head sagged. "Larry's already confessed. I just wanted to hear the story from you."

We got in her car and took a little drive.

Down the road a bit, I asked, "So what did Larry tell you?"

"He said you and he have made love a couple of times in his van. He said it didn't mean anything to him, that you both felt horrible, and that it was over." She looked at me for a reaction and then continued. "He promised me he would never speak to you or see you again."

Only the Heart Know's...

I couldn't believe what she was saying! *How could he do this? He just told me thirty minutes ago how much he loved me!* I just sat there in a state of shock and disbelief. She kept talking and talking, but I couldn't comprehend what she was saying. *How could Larry do this to me after all the time we'd spent together, after all the times he'd told me he couldn't live without me, and after he'd said over and over that he loved me? How am I going to get through this without him?* Suddenly I felt all alone—abandoned.

I shook my head to clear my thoughts, and I slowly began telling her the harsh truth. She deserved the truth, and so did I.

I handed her my cell phone and told her to pull up all the calls he had made to me in the last few days. I think it was over twenty. I told her about the apartment, the hotels, and some of the gifts. I also told her I'd fought my feelings and emotions for Larry a very long time, but that he had been very persistent. I told her we had been in love for almost two years. There was so much to tell—so much I wanted to share—but it seemed useless. She dropped me off at home.

I went in and told my husband, and of course he was shell-shocked. I told him it was over and that after this evening I would tell him everything. Then I got ready for my dinner.

The fundraising dinner was a huge success. It went off even better then planned. We made the front page of the newspaper the next day, and everyone thought everything was perfect … except me. I was lost.

Chapter 28
The Impact

I had attempted to live my life backwards. I tried to have someone in my life in order to be happier. I think the way it actually works is the reverse of that. You have to be who you really are, then do what you need to do in order to have whom you want in your life. Larry and I should have cleared the way first and done everything right. Then maybe things would've turned out differently for everyone. My thirst for happiness had clouded my reasoning and my heart.

It felt like a nuclear bomb had just gone off in my life. The impact of what I had done with Larry was nothing less than horrible. I was suffering, and my husband was racked with sorrow and pain. There was nothing I could do but take responsibility for the miserable things I had done. The pain, embarrassment, and emptiness I felt from the affair were overwhelming. Patrick was relentless in his punishment. His anger would take him completely over, and his moods would swing from bad to worse. He didn't know how to handle his pain, and sometimes he would take it out on me physically and emotionally, but I never once denied my feelings and love for Larry. To do so would have been much worse for my soul. I did love him. It had taken me time to fall in love with him, but once I did, I loved him with all my heart and soul and spirit. As for Larry, I couldn't say. I think he charmed and lied his way out of his part of the affair with Agnes. I truly don't know. Only he could answer for what he had done.

My neighbors, John and Kelly, who had known all along what was going on and had actually encouraged the relationship, came over to my house the day after the news broke about the affair. I was rolled up in a ball in one of my silk chairs next to the fireplace. I was visibly shaken, broken, and grief stricken. As I sat there with tears running down my cheeks, they wanted to make sure I would never divulge what they knew and when they'd known it. Point blank. They just wanted to exonerate themselves from any responsibility they felt over the whole affair.

When John was finished making his point clear to protect his wife from Agnes, Kelly asked whether she could have a few minutes alone with me for some girl talk.

Only the Heart Know's...

John agreed and said, "Laura, I never in a million years thought Larry would choose to stay with Agnes. I'm so sorry. You know I love you like a sister." Then he gave me a hug and left.

Kelly came over to me and said she understood everything I was going through. She explained that a few summers earlier, she and John had been having a rough time of it; their marriage had been in trouble. She went on to say that she and Larry had been very intimate and that it seemed for a while that they, too, were in love. She said Larry understood her and had made her feel like she meant everything to him; he had made her feel good about herself. She winked and said, "In time you'll begin to feel better. This sadness will pass. You weren't the first, nor will you be the last. Larry is a predator. He enjoys the kill."

I looked up at her in disbelief. She hugged me and gave me another tissue, and then she was gone. *So she had a love affair with Larry too!* I thought. *Well, he is a car salesman. He's charming, crafty, and greedy. How did I ever fall for this guy? I have to get over him and all of his lies.* My grandmother used to say "If you roll around with pigs, you're going to get dirty." *Well guess what, Grandmother? I've been rolling around with the king pig, and I'm really dirty and ashamed. Please pray for me and help me out of this mess!*

Just then that I remembered the saying "What doesn't kill you makes you stronger." I knew that if I lived through this, I'd be strong as steel. Love, hope, and forgiveness were what I needed.

I found myself at a crossroads. Rather then taking the path of least resistance, I decided to work on my family and myself. I started to give trust again through everyday life. God closed some doors and opened lots of windows to let in plenty of sunlight and a soft, scented breeze. This cleansed my spirit and my soul. I picked up the pieces and began my life again … there was hope.

After six months of therapy, prayer, and talks with my priest, I forgave myself. My merciful God forgave me too. I get the feeling that God loves to give people second chances, especially if they are truly sorry in their hearts. I know that I didn't go looking for sin, but sin surely found me. I am truly sorry for hurting so many people. An affair can have a lasting effect on your life. I decided that I would try to move forward and learn from my mistakes. All I wanted was love and all I got was pain. I'm not sorry for loving; I'm sorry for not waiting to do everything right—the way it is intended.

Epilogue

Larry has returned to his old life. He is back with his obsessive-compulsive wife. I heard through the grapevine that they are spending a lot of time at church and marriage counseling. I think that could be good thing. Maybe if they really listen to each other they will hear the truth. Agnes may admit the mean and hateful things she used to say about Larry while not ever really loving him, but rather just settling for him. Larry may confess that he finds her repulsive, boring, and most importantly, lazy. I know that together they have done some unscrupulous things to make money. That is the glue that holds them together. He has been afraid that she will blow the whistle on him and that he will get into a lot of trouble—maybe even jail time. I see now that they deserve each other. Besides, Agnes always did put way too much value on materialism. I'm sure that after the dust settles, Larry will be back in business again, looking for another unsuspecting lonely lady. He will always be a predator.

As for my dear friend Kathryn, who is also a victim to Larry's lies and betrayals, she too had been convinced by him that he was in love with her and that they were going to get married and live happily ever after. She is having a harder time adjusting to life without Larry. He dropped her just as quickly as he did me. The big difference is that she is completely alone. Kathryn doesn't have any children. Both her father and brother have passed away from cancer. Her surviving mother has Alzheimer's disease. She has found herself completely alone. Sadly, the loss of Larry's love has affected her tremendously. Depression is taking its toll on my sweet friend. She has her flight attendant job and a few good friends, including me.

One day she came over to my house. Kathryn just wanted to stare over at Larry's house, perhaps to get a glimpse of Agnes or Larry .Much to her surprise, she did! She saw Agnes! She could not believe her eyes! "How sad," she said. "I think now I understand why he strayed." But she still didn't understand how she could be tricked or conned, especially by someone she loved. After a few hours of watching Agnes mow the lawn and a couple glasses of wine, Kathryn and I talked out our times with Larry .We laughed and then we cried. After all that, we decided that God saved us from Larry, all the darkness, and the pain.

Being alive is a grand thing. Love is the ultimate power we have to give one another. I had grown in strength and courage. Perhaps loving someone is only the starting place; perhaps I'll make a better life for myself after all. Larry abandoned me—left me holding the bag, so to speak. Maybe he was a coward, or maybe he was just a big baby filled with fear. Whatever his reasons were for slithering away after all of his chasing and pursuing, only he could answer for them. As for me, it just felt good to have an end to this journey one way or another. It is the journey itself with Larry that I will cherish and keep in my heart. The only two people who can really share the memories are Larry and myself. If I had the chance to do it all over again, would I? I don't know. Would you?

Oh yes, I'm living a wonderful, full life. It has taken time, but I've endured great love and great sorrow. I have a beautiful little boy whom I adore. I have heartfelt memories to share with my family and friends. God had shown me a few miracles too. The library is being finished thanks to grants and kind people in the community. Just being alive is a miracle in itself. I don't know what the future will be for Patrick and me. We are on neutral ground; maybe we will find each other again and fall in love.

I think I'm ready to embark on a new and exciting path. Perhaps a new career—an adventure that's fun and exciting. Or maybe if Patrick and I call it quits ... hmm,

Adam is out there somewhere ... maybe he didn't get married. Hmm ...my Greek god! I just might get that kick back in my step!

When I'm an old lady and my granddaughter asks me about life and love, I will tell her that I was once in love with a dirty little white boy and that I wouldn't have missed loving him for the world. Embrace your life, love, and loss. Grow and learn from everything. Remember, only your heart knows for sure.

Printed in the United States
80434LV00001B/37-84